W9-CMD-423

A SECRET,
A SAFARI,
A SECOND CHANCE

A SECRET,
A SAFARI,
A SECOND CHANCE

LIZ FIELDING

MILLS & BOON

First published in Great Britain 2019
by Mills & Boon, an imprint of HarperCollins*Publishers*
1 London Bridge Street, London, SE1 9GF

Large Print edition 2020

© 2019 Liz Fielding

ISBN: 978-0-263-08408-5

Printed and bound in Great Britain
by CPI Group (UK) Ltd, Croydon, CR0 4YY

For Donna, Barbara and Nina,
with whom I have shared great hugs,
both in cyberspace and in reality.
Forever friends.

PROLOGUE

'ARE YOU COLD, RED?'

Eve was shivering, but the Nantucket evening was balmy; the cold was coming from inside.

She'd been cajoled into joining this beach party by the older women in her family, who were worried about her and thought she needed to get out, assuring her kindly that some young company would 'cheer her up'.

Her cousins, given no choice in the matter, had done their best to include her, but these teenagers had known one another all their lives. She was twenty-one, in her last year at university; they all seemed so young, and her novelty value as 'the English cousin' was outweighed by the awkwardness of the fact that her mother had just died.

Bit of a downer, that.

She'd taken pity on them, pleading a headache to move away from the music and the bonfire to sit in the quiet shadow of the dunes, welcoming the chance to be on her own for a while, without having family fussing around her. Counting down the time until her grandmother would be in bed and she could slip back into the house, so that she wouldn't have to pretend to have had a good time.

So that her grandmother wouldn't have to pretend to care.

The last thing she needed was for someone to hit on her.

'If I lend you my sweater can I join your escape party?' She managed to stuff the little soft elephant she'd been cradling for comfort out of sight in her bag but, before she could tell the guy to get lost, he had draped a soft cashmere sweater across her shoulders and flopped down beside her on the sand. The sweater smelled not of woodsmoke but of the sea and, as her body relaxed into its soft warmth, she didn't shake it off but pulled it around her.

'Hi,' he said, offering a large, square hand. 'I'm Kit.' Years at an English boarding school had drummed in the automatic 'politeness' response but as she reached up to take it, her own name died in her throat.

She might only be an occasional summer

visitor to her mother's birthplace, but everyone knew Kit Merchant. An island legend, he'd
been a teenager when he'd brought home sailing gold from London and had been collecting
trophies ever since.

Now in his mid-twenties, he was too old, and
a lot too glamorous, to be hanging out at a teen-
age beach party.

'This isn't a party,' she said, but curiosity beat
her irritation that he'd called her Red. Her hair,
a gift from her mother's Scottish ancestors, had
been an unending source of nicknames ever
since she'd gone to school and it had got old.
'What are you escaping from?'

Without taking his eyes off her, or letting go
of her hand, he waved in the general direction
of the fun on the beach. 'It's my kid sister's
birthday and I've been appointed the responsible adult.'

'Oh, bad luck.'

'Not that bad if I can sit it out with you?'

He had to be kidding but the guy was not
only a legend, he was over-the-top gorgeous
from his tousled hair to his long, bare feet. Suddenly, being on her own felt overrated.

'Is that what a responsible adult would do?' she asked.

'I've given them the "no booze, no sex" talk and, since they were polite enough not to laugh, I thought I'd retreat to a safe distance so that they can enjoy themselves.'

The flames of the bonfire were reflected in his eyes, dancing off his cheeks, adding golden highlights to his sun-silvered hair and she felt warmed, not just by his sweater, but his smile.

'In other words, no.'

'My responsibility extends to all my sister's guests, especially the ones sitting on their own looking sad. So, who are you? And why are you hiding out over here when you could be having fun drinking soda and toasting marshmallows?'

Despite the smile, there was an edge to 'having fun' that suggested he was having a bad evening, too. That neither of them wanted to be here.

'I hate soda,' she said, 'and my marshmallows always fall into the fire.'

Her name she kept to herself. Her mother's memorial service had been all over the local papers and if she told him that she was Gene-vieve Bliss, the flirtatious mood would shatter.

It felt like a lifetime since she'd smiled, since she'd been treated with anything other than kid gloves, let alone flirted with and, choosing not to be that 'poor girl' whose mother had died of a fever in a Central American jungle, she took her cue from him.

'Red is good enough and, like you, I'm too old for this party.'

He looked at her for a moment then with what might have been a shrug said, 'In that case, Red, can I tempt you to a decent bottle of wine and I'm sure to have something a little more substantial than marshmallows in the fridge?'

'You have a fridge?' She lifted a disbeliev-ing brow and he laughed.

'I not only have a fridge,' he said, 'I have a cabin just down the beach.'

'What about the party?'

He looked across at the young people sit-ting around in groups, chatting, drinking soda. One or two were dancing to music that reached them as little more than a bass beat. He hesi-tated for a moment, then said, 'If they need me, they know where to find me.'

Could this be real? She was being invited by a world-famous yachtsman, a man whose face and ripped body had appeared on countless magazine covers, to have supper with him in a cabin on the beach?

Sensing her own hesitation, he said, 'I'm not hitting on you, Scout's honour.'

He sounded serious, but his eyes were telling a different story, his mouth was temptingly close and she was overwhelmed by a reckless need to be held, to be warm again.

'How disappointing,' she said, and his sweater slipped from her shoulders as she hooked her free hand around the back of his head. For a moment neither of them moved and then, as she closed her eyes, he kissed her.

CHAPTER ONE

Nearly four years later

'ARE YOU COLD, HONEY?'

Genevieve Bliss was shivering, but not with the cold. She had been on edge from the moment she'd arrived on Nantucket and tonight's charity dinner and auction to raise funds for an opioid clinic was not helping.

It wasn't the cause. She knew the clinic was desperately needed. It was the location. The Merchant Seafarer Resort was the last place she would have chosen to visit voluntarily, but her godmother, recovering from a hip replacement and pleading the need of her arm, was determined to bid at the auction.

'I'm fine,' she said, forcing herself to relax as they approached the impressive entrance.

It would be fine.

Kit Merchant, according to his team blog, was on the other side of the world putting a new multimillion-pound racing yacht through its paces. Even if he was here, he wouldn't recognise a girl who, for one unforgettable night, he'd called Red.

Not that she believed for one moment that it had been unforgettable for him. His playboy reputation was a gift to the gossip magazines and without the red hair to flag up a reminder, she would be lost in the crowd both literally and figuratively.

'I'm just a little overawed to be honest, Martha,' she said, as they made their way to the cloakroom. 'This place is way out of my comfort zone.'

'To be brutally frank, Eve, I'd say your comfort zone and your wardrobe are both overdue a serious shake-up.'

On the contrary, what she'd gone for was a shake-down.

Desperate to hide the red hair that could be seen from a mile away, just in case he made a flying trip home, she'd used a semi-permanent colour to tone it down. She'd been aiming for something approaching the glossy brunette on the carton; her hair had resisted the transformation and what she'd ended up with was a muddy brown.

It wasn't pretty, and it had been a shock to catch sight of herself in a mirror, but it was temporary, and she could live with it. Her dress was, she had to admit, not flattering.

She hadn't brought party clothes with her; it hadn't been that kind of visit. Even if there had been room in her bag after she'd packed for Hannah, she wouldn't have trusted the zipper on anything in her wardrobe.

Ghastly hair and the extra pounds were, she told herself, the perfect camouflage. If, by any chance, she was to pass Kit Merchant in the street, he wouldn't notice her, let alone take a second look.

If she were with Hannah on the other hand...

Far away in London, it had been easy to convince herself that she'd done the right thing. Here, where the Merchant name was everywhere, she wasn't so certain.

'Where on earth did you get that dress?' Martha asked, as she took off her coat.

'You really aren't helping my self-confidence, Martha,' she said as, attempting to make a joke of it, she struck a pose. 'This dress is a classic.'

At her godmother's raised eyebrow, she said, 'Honest. I found it in Nana's wardrobe. She'd never even worn it. It still had the tags.'

Martha was not amused. 'The last time your grandmother bought a new dress Reagan was president.'

'It's lovely material.'

'It fits where it touches. At your age you should be shaking out the red curls Mother Nature gave you and wearing something outrageous to go with that tattoo you're so desperate to keep hidden.'

'A moment of graduation madness,' she said, turning around to try and catch a glimpse in the cloakroom mirror. 'I didn't realise it showed.' She tugged at the dress. 'I need to lose those last few pounds of baby weight before I wear anything likely to scare the horses.'

'Nonsense. Hidden beneath that shapeless sack of a dress you have a lovely figure.'

As Martha, unable to disguise her irritation, shook her own head, the pink streak in her sharply angled silver bob caught the light. A picture of elegance right down to her silver-topped Malacca cane, Eve's seventy-year-old godmother made her look like a dreary governess in some nineteenth-century novel.

'You were the loveliest girl, Eve, and somewhere, hiding beneath your grandmother's dress and a very bad hair colour, is a beautiful young woman. What on earth were you thinking?'

'The dress or the hair?'

She waved a dismissive hand. 'You can take off the dress and the sooner the better. Your hair is another matter altogether.'

'My hair was all anybody ever saw,' she said, capturing a wayward curl that no amount of hairspray could ever quite control, pinning it on automatic, implying that the change had happened long ago and had nothing to do with her visit to Nantucket. 'People didn't ask my name, they just called me Red.' Not true, only one person had ever called her Red, but there had been other names. Coppernob, Carrots, Clown. 'And I don't think the head of a prestigious boys' school would employ a science teacher who dressed outrageously.'

'Don't tell me you're planning to live with that look permanently if you get the job?'

She'd worn a conservative grey suit and

pinned her hair up as tight as humanly possible for the interview and had somehow reached the shortlist. It had been the perfect excuse to keep her visit to her ailing grandmother as short as possible.

The best-laid plans...

'I had to call them when Nana died to let them know that I wouldn't be available for a second interview.'

'Surely, under the circumstances, they would have waited?'

'They could have held the post for another week, but the cottage was an unforeseen complication,' she said. 'Since I couldn't give them a date, I had to step down.'

'You weren't expecting to inherit your grandmother's cottage?' Martha asked, surprised.

After the way she'd left, she wouldn't have been surprised if Nana had left it to her cat. The creature was old, bad-tempered, and the rest of the family had, as one, taken a sharp step back when she'd raised the question of re-homing him.

'I didn't inherit it,' she pointed out. 'Nana left it, and everything in it, in trust for Hannah.'

The lawyers had made it plain that her plan

to invite the family to help themselves to furniture and anything else they wanted, get a firm in to clear out what was left and leave it in the hands of a realtor, was not an option.

'I should probably sympathise with the lost opportunity,' Martha said, 'but good teachers are always in demand. You can't sell the cottage, but you and Hannah could live there. Stay on the island and let your hair grow out. Someone has to take care of that cat,' she added.

With the summer approaching, Eve had to admit that it did sound a lot more appealing than going back to supply teaching in London. Apart from the cat.

Unfortunately, Hannah's father wouldn't stay in the southern hemisphere for ever, forcing her to face the decision she'd been avoiding for so long that it now felt...impossible.

And she wouldn't be able to hide behind the muddy brown for ever.

She'd be for ever on edge, never knowing when she might turn a corner, with not just hers but Hannah's unmissable bright red curls blazing in the sunlight, and find herself face-to-face with the man who'd lived up to his reputation as a serial love 'em and leave 'em playboy.

'Once I've sorted out the family stuff and put it into storage I'm going to freshen up the cottage and put it on the rental market to build up a college fund for Hannah,' she said, aware that Kit Merchant wasn't the only one on the run.

'Or you could sublet your London flat and put that money in the bank,' Martha pointed out. 'Unless there's some pressing reason to return to London? You never talk about Hannah's father. Does he support her? Does she see him?'

'N-no—' It would have been the perfect excuse, but then she would have had to invent some man, a relationship that had gone off the rails. She'd told Hannah that she didn't see her father because he lived in another country but that he had been kind when her mama had been very sad.

Her best friend at preschool had a daddy who lived in Australia so she'd accepted it without question.

For now.

She knew that if Hannah was ever to know who her father was, she would have to tell Kit, but she was very afraid that he wouldn't want to know.

'He was there at a bad moment,' she told Martha. 'That's all.'

True, and less embarrassing than admitting that her precious daughter was the result of a one-night stand at a beach party with her mother's ashes barely in the ground.

Shame had sent her running back to England and then a pregnancy that would have caused gossip, raised eyebrows, a stain on her mother's memory, had kept her away.

Her daughter had turned three at the beginning of May, time enough, she hoped, for dates to have blurred.

'Did you ever tell him about Hannah?' Martha asked.

'I... No,' she admitted. 'He was long gone before she arrived.'

To say that Martha pulled a face would have been an exaggeration. There was the slightest movement of muscles, more than enough to show her disapproval. 'And now you're hiding out, afraid to get involved again.'

'It's simpler this way.'

'Men do tend to complicate life,' Martha agreed, 'but they add a little spice. You're a single mother, Eve, not a nun.'

'Martha! I'm shocked.'

'Are you?' Her godmother could write an essay with the lift of an eyebrow. 'Clearly you haven't heard the rumour that it was my generation that invented sex as a recreational pastime.'

It was perhaps as well that, having arrived at the entrance to the ballroom, Martha didn't wait for a response, but reached for a glass of champagne.

'This is stunning,' Eve said, following suit as she took in the magnificence of the ivory-and-gold ballroom.

She'd never been to the resort as a girl, although she'd instantly recognised Kit Merchant when he'd left the party to come and talk to her.

She hadn't wanted to talk, and she was pretty sure he hadn't followed her for the conversation. A local hero, he could probably have had any girl on the beach, but they were his kid sister's friends, pretty and no doubt keen to attract his attention. Trouble, in fact, which might have accounted for his eagerness to get away.

Normally, she'd have told him to get lost, but she'd been a mess. Her mother had just died, and her father hadn't felt the need to fly in to support her at the funeral. Her boyfriend had felt the same way, sticking to his plan to go backpacking around Europe during the spring break rather than fly to Nantucket, and she'd dumped him by text from the airport.

She'd been at the party because her cousins' arms had been twisted to take her with them and she had only gone to get away from another miserable night sitting in with Nana.

She had been desperate for someone, anyone, to put their arms around her, to hold her, and Kit had been in the wrong place at the wrong time.

Not that he'd failed her. Far from it. No doubt used to females throwing themselves at him, he had responded with some truly outstanding sex. Not the wham, bam, anonymous stuff she'd expected, had wanted right there on the beach to drive away the pain. Instead he'd grabbed her hand, racing with her to his beach hut where they'd had hot, mindless sex, as if they were both desperate to blot out the world. But then he had slowed everything down. They had drunk a rich red wine under a star-filled sky before making slow, sweet love; the kind that could break your heart. That you would never forget.

She swallowed, looking at the men in dinner jackets, the women in their beautiful clothes, and had a moment of regret for the head-turning red curls, wishing she were wearing something a little less...classic.

Wanting, just for a moment, to feel that alive again.

But only for a moment.

She'd been there and done that. She had Hannah, with her own Titian curls and Kit's bright blue eyes, as a constant reminder of the night she'd lost her head.

Her baby girl. The love of her life.

She knew she should tell him, that he had a right to know, but her world was complicated enough. She wasn't going to stick around and risk blundering into the man who'd made her laugh, made her cry, made love to her with a sweet passion that had changed everything in one starlit night.

The man who, at the fierce banging on his beach cabin door, the call that he was needed, had rolled out of bed, pulling on his jeans and grabbing his sweatshirt. All he'd said was, 'Stay out of sight...' on his way out.

She had waited until the first pink edge of dawn appeared on the horizon and then she had run back to her grandmother's house and thrown her things into a bag. Nana had been asleep, so she'd left a note, caught the first ferry back to the mainland and been back in London twenty-four hours later.

Had he waited, holding his breath, waiting for the call from one of the less glossy gossip mags asking for a comment on the story they were about to run?

My Night of Sex... Sex in the Sand... Abandoned After a Night of Sex...

There had been stories in the past and, even if some of them were pure fiction and others heavily embellished to make better headlines, he had clearly made the most of his youthful fame. There were still photographs of him with beautiful women, but these days no one was talking, and neither would she. Not even when, weeks later, after her finals were over, she'd had time to realise what was happening to her body and two pink lines had changed her life for ever.

She hadn't talked and she couldn't call Kit.

The news had been full of the start of the single-handed round-the-world yacht race, or maybe that was all she had been noticing because Kit was the skipper that every camera had been watching, the man already making the headlines after rumours that his entry had caused a rift with his family.

Calling him on the satellite link would have been a very public way to inform him that he was about to become a father. While the headlines would have cheered a newspaper man's heart and set Twitter alight, the trolls would have been out in force. She would have been mobbed by the press, her poor grandmother would have been under siege, and she would have had to go into hiding.

It had given her plenty of time to think. Time for her heart to stop when, two months into the race, his radio had gone silent after a storm. She'd hugged her belly protectively during the ten long days before he'd been spotted by search aircraft.

The photographs had shown that his damaged mast had been lashed back into place and the pundits had speculated with sickening detail how he must have climbed in heavy seas to repair it.

Worse, he'd signalled that his communication equipment had been smashed in the storm that hit his mast, but he was okay and was continuing with the race.

He'd finally limped home after more than four months in third place. A great feat of sailing, according to the yachting community.

Eve hadn't cared about the sailing or the press, she'd just been furious that he would recklessly endanger himself for a piece of silverware to stick on the mantelpiece.

Had he no feelings for his family and what they must have gone through?

She knew all about recklessness. Her mother had taken risks and died; she would protect the precious little girl growing inside her from that kind of pain.

'Kit? Where are you?'

'Sorry, sis. The ferry was late but we should be with you in about thirty minutes.'

'We could delay the start—'

'No, dinner won't wait so go ahead with the presentations. Lucy can speak after dinner before the serious bidding. How was Dad this evening?'

'Furious. Frustrated at not being able to remember stuff. To walk properly. To say what he's thinking.'

'That's probably a blessing.'

Laura laughed. 'Undoubtedly, but he's improving every day, even if the words aren't in any dictionary, so stand back to have your ears blasted.'

'Your grandmother and I used to come here all the time when we were growing up,' Martha said. 'Christmas parties, birthday treats, sailing. I missed her so much when she went off on her travels after college.'

'I didn't know Nana travelled. Where did she go?'

'Spain, France, Italy, Ireland. There are photographs. You'll find them as you sort through the cottage. Bring them over and I'll tell you who everyone is.' She sighed. 'The itchy-feet gene runs deep in your family. Your mother was away to Africa on some research trip the moment the ink was dry on her degree, met your father and never really came home again.'

'Nana wasn't...'

'Welcoming? Easy to live with?' Martha finished for her. 'She was such fun as a girl, but she was never the same after your grandfather died. We tried to involve her, but we didn't understand so much about depression back then and we were all so busy with our own families.' She shook her head. 'But that's not what kept your mother on the move. That's who she was. I've never been further than Boston, which is why she asked me to be your godmother. She wanted someone grounded in your life.'

Eve struggled for something to say but Martha rescued her.

'I thought you were going to follow in your parents' footsteps, Eve. I seem to recall that you were studying zoology?'

'I was.' She had dreamed of returning to Africa, to the scent of hot earth when the rains came, the thunder of hoofbeats as a million wildebeest migrated across the plains, velvet-black skies filled with stars. 'When I discovered I was pregnant I realised that fieldwork wasn't going to be an option, at least not for me, so I forgot about my Masters and I took a teaching diploma.'

'Pregnancy didn't slow your mother down.'

'She wasn't alone, not until Dad left her, but I'd never send Hannah to boarding school.'

Martha reached out and took her hand. 'Her death was such a tragedy. I hope your little girl gives you some comfort.'

'She is a gift, Martha. My joy.'

'Well, let's hope this visit will be as blessed,' Martha said, innocently.

Eve realised that she'd underestimated her godmother's capacity for mental arithmetic, but she'd been away on a fishing trip when Eve had met Kit that summer. Martha might have put her swift departure together with Hannah's birthday and come up with a theory about where and when, but that was all it was. There was no way she could be certain that Hannah had been conceived on the island.

'People are beginning to sit down,' she said, changing the subject. 'Shall we go and find our table?'

Martha knew everyone at their table, mostly couples of her own generation who greeted her warmly before quietening to listen to Barbara Merchant welcome them and introduce the auction.

She had the same colouring as Kit, Eve thought; the same sun-streaked hair, the same vivid blue eyes. Lost in memories of that night, she heard little of her introduction to the cause for which the auction was being held.

'Let's go and check out the trips,' Martha said, when she was done.

Monitors showed film of the trips on offer at Merchant resorts and some of their partners, in fabulous locations.

There was whale watching off the west coast, trips to Europe—vineyards in France, culture in Italy, golfing and fishing in Scotland—but it was the last one, the wildlife safari, that brought a gasp to Eve's lips.

The Nymba Safari Lodge had been built high amongst the trees with viewing platforms where you could watch animals in a landscape that was painfully familiar. There was a glimpse of a giraffe at sunset, forelegs spreadeagled as it drank at the oxbow lake. There was the dusty green bark of fever trees, a family of warthogs snuffling through the grass.

'Eve?'

'Nymba... It was our home,' she said. 'It's where we lived...'

The cover of the brochure for the safari trip had a photograph of a mama elephant, trunk curled protectively around her calf, and Eve picked it up, instinctively hugging it to her.

Nymba...

It was what her mother had called their *boma*. The word meant home and for just a moment she could hear her mother's voice as she'd given her a hug before putting a small grey velvet elephant in her arms and sending her off to school.

'This little elephant's trunk is my arm, Evie. Hold onto it when you're lost...put it around you when you need a hug...'

She wished she could wind the clock back to those last few weeks with her.

'Excuse me? Can I get in there?'

The woman waited for her to move and Eve stepped back, forcing a smile as she turned to Martha.

'There are some really exciting trips on offer. Have you seen anything you like?' she asked.

'I was hoping for something a little more relaxing than zip-lining through a rainforest,' she said, 'but this one could have been made for you. Your grandmother left you some money and you could do with a break.'

'That's rainy-day money and, anyway, Hannah is too young to come with me.'

'The rule with an inheritance is to give ten per cent, save ten per cent and spend the rest,' Martha said. 'Serendipitously, if you were to make a winning bid for the safari, you'd be economising by giving and spending at the same time.'

Eve laughed at her logic but shook her head. 'Good try, but I couldn't leave Hannah.'

'It's only for ten days. I don't imagine you took her to lectures with you when she was a baby? Teaching practice?'

'Well, no. Obviously. She is in a wonderful day nursery, but I've never left her at night. She'd miss me.' And she knew everything there was to know about missing your mother.

'Mary would love to have her stay and Hannah would have a great time with her cousins.'

'You're very free with your daughter's hospitality.'

But Eve knew her godmother was right.

Mary was one of those women who wrapped you up in a hug and instantly made the world seem a better place. Older, she'd been married and living in New York when Eve's mother had died, or things might have been very different.

Now she and her husband were back on the island with their three children and a menagerie of pets, and Hannah adored, and was adored by, all of them. Every sentence seemed to begin with Cara and Jason and Lacey...

'Okay,' she admitted. 'I'd miss *her*.' Putting an end to the discussion, she turned to a rail journey across the US. 'This hits the less strenuous requirement,' she said. 'Or how about this camel trek across the desert? Camping out under the stars. You might meet a dark-eyed sheikh. Very romantic.'

'There is nothing in the least bit romantic about camels, Eve. They spit.'

'Okay... Is there anything here that you do fancy?'

'I'm rather taken with the idea of sailing down the Adriatic from Venice to the Greek islands in that classic nineteenth-century sailing yacht, and if Kit Merchant happened to be at the helm there would always be something attractive to look at.'

Eve felt her cheeks heat at the mention of his name. 'Isn't he estranged from his family?'

'There was a big row three or four years ago. Christopher didn't want him to take part in the round-the-world race. He said it was time to stop playing and concentrate on the business.'

'Sailing is his life.'

'The resort is his father's.'

Eve had to clear her throat, stop herself from looking around, although she suddenly felt as if she had a great big sign on her back saying 'HERE' before she could manage a bright, 'Maybe a brush with death will soften his father's attitude.'

'Maybe. Ah, now this is the one I've been looking for.' Martha picked up a pen, wrote her name and a substantial bid for a vacation at the Merchant Spa in Phuket. Then she held out the pen. 'Your turn.'

Eve looked back at the African trip.

'Just to show my support,' she said, raising a fairly modest bid that someone had already made.

She had only just put down the pen when a man picked it up and outbid her.

Martha had met someone she knew and, while she was talking, Eve checked by how much she'd been outbid. Five hundred dollars…

It was still ridiculously cheap, and she placed another bid.

Just to help push up the price.

She straightened to find Martha, thoughtful, watching and guiltily put down the pen. 'It's going to go much higher.'

'They're starting to serve dinner,' she said. 'We should go back to our table.'

As they moved away someone else stepped up to make another bid. As Eve smothered a squeak of protest, Martha took her arm.

'Leave it until after dinner when we know what we're up against.'

'Yes... No!' Realising how quickly she'd been sucked in, she said, 'Wow, that's dangerous.'

'The trick is to decide on your top bid and not to get carried away. Well, not too much,' Martha added, smiling.

'Oh, no, I'm done,' Eve declared, but she couldn't stop herself from looking back, fingers twitching.

CHAPTER TWO

THE FOOD WAS EXCELLENT, the company—if more her godmother's generation than her own—was interesting and the wine flowed freely enough that she was pleasantly relaxed by the time Barbara Merchant returned to the stage.

'Hi, yes, sorry it's me again but this is a charity dinner and you all knew you'd have to dig deep, right? Has everyone bought raffle tickets?' There was a murmur from the room and she said, 'Well, buy some more! We'll be drawing some amazing prizes very soon.' She paused a moment for the laughter to die down, then said, 'Before you all rush to spend money on a good cause, and to tell you why this fundraiser is so important, I'd like you to welcome my son, Kit, who, after his father's stroke, has come home to give us all his support.'

Eve was only half listening, her thoughts focussed on the past, and, not sure she'd heard right, she turned to look and there he was, standing beside his mother.

'Kit?'

The word was little more than a whisper but Martha leaned over and said, 'Word is that he's resigned as skipper of the Cup team.'

Before she could take that in, Barbara Merchant said, 'I'll leave Kit to introduce his friend and fellow sailor who has come all the way from New Zealand to tell you why this clinic is so desperately needed.'

This couldn't be happening. She'd checked the team's blog before she left for Nantucket, just to be sure. There had been a photograph of him, taken less than a month ago, at the helm of the new yacht he and his team were putting through its paces in the Southern Ocean.

Even as her mind was rejecting the possibility that he was not simply in Nantucket but in this very room, Kit Merchant's low, baritone voice reached out across the space and touched her like a lover's caress.

'Ladies and gentlemen, friends...'

For a moment Eve couldn't breathe, couldn't move...

And then the reality of his mother's introduction, Martha's whispered comment, sank in. This wasn't a flying visit, Kit was back, if not for good, then for the foreseeable future.

'My mother has already thanked our generous partners throughout the world who have joined Merchant Resorts to offer thrilling, one-off experiences for this auction, but events such as this do not organise themselves...'

Every cell in her body was warning her to keep absolutely still; she was afraid that any movement would attract his attention, draw his gaze in her direction.

And then what?

From that distance all he would see was a badly dressed woman with mousy hair. The kind of woman who wouldn't hold his attention for a second.

She'd seen his face on a hundred magazine covers in the years since their encounter on the beach. She knew the exact shade of blue of his eyes, knew each line weathered into his face by sun, saltwater and wind, the shape of the close-trimmed beard that he'd grown. She knew the way his thick, sun-streaked hair stuck up as if he'd just dragged his hand through it. As if she had just dragged her hand through it.

It had been just one night, but she could still feel the soft thickness of it beneath her own fingers, still knew the taste of his lips, the sweet murmur of his voice, the scent of sharp, clean sweat on his skin.

'...thank those of you who have given your time to help my mother and sister organise this amazing auction.'

She wanted to slide from her chair, curl up and hide beneath the table but she was frozen, unable to look away as, oblivious to her presence, he was turning to the lovely young woman standing beside him.

'Before you all rush to top up your bids,' he said, 'I want to introduce Lucy Grainger. Along with her brother Matt, she was a member of my crew. Matt was my first mate, my best mate, a friend, a brother from a different mother, who died last year. This auction is because of his death...'

As he stepped back Kit's eyes swept the room and for a moment, one brief shocking moment, they came to rest on her.

It was as if he could see through the brown dye to the red curls desperately trying to burst out of the clamped-down chignon. As if he could see through the boring dress to the body that she had once, desperately, thrown at him and which he had caught so deftly.

Relief came as he stepped back to leave Lucy in the spotlight and, as if released from some unseen force field, her breath could finally escape, allowing her body to sag as the tension left her.

'Eve? Are you okay?' Martha whispered.

'I'm a bit warm. The wine...' She shook her head when Martha suggested some fresh air, not wanting to draw attention to herself. She could slip away as soon as everyone made a move. 'I'll be fine.'

She sipped a glass of water as the young woman told the audience about her brother, Matt, a gifted international yachtsman like Kit, who'd hidden an injury so that he could continue competing and, as a result, had become addicted to painkillers. First prescription and then later, when they stopped working, to stronger and stronger drugs bought on the Internet and finally from the streets.

She was young, beautiful, there were tears in her eyes as she spoke of his kindness, his talent, and when she'd finished speaking Kit put his arms around her and held her, giving her a moment to recover before leading her from the stage.

She'd seen photographs of him with a dozen beautiful women, but this was different. There was a tenderness here that had been lacking in those posed shots. This girl was different.

It shouldn't matter.

He'd been her comfort in a bleak moment, in the wrong place at the wrong time. It wasn't just his recklessness, a complete disregard for his life, that had stopped her from calling him.

It had been a magical evening, a precious moment in a dark time, and she hadn't wanted to destroy that memory. It wasn't as if he was going to say, my bad, our child needs a father, marry me. No one did that any more and she'd read about too many cases in which the rich and famous had defended paternity suits through the courts, with every sordid detail aired for the world to salivate over.

She hadn't needed his money.

She'd had the London flat and divorce settlement, left to her in her mother's will. She'd had a career—science teachers were in short supply and she would never be short of a job. She and Hannah would be fine.

She'd thought it would be easy. She'd thought she would never see him again.

But there he was.

And it did matter.

'Give me a hand up, Eve,' Martha said. 'I've sat too long and seized up, but I'm determined not to be outbid.'

Grabbing the chance to escape, she said, 'Would you like me to bid for you?'

'And miss all the fun? Come on. Let's see how we're doing.'

There were more people around the bidding forms now, checking to see if they were in with a chance, making last-minute bids. Martha pulled a face and went higher.

'Is that your limit?' Eve asked, hoping to get away.

'My limit and more,' she admitted. 'Come on. It's your turn.'

There were half a dozen bids after hers and while she was looking up at the display someone took it up another two hundred and fifty dollars.

Nymba…

Home.

As she hesitated, torn between longing and reality, there was a movement at the far end of the table as Kit and Lucy arrived to chat to the bidders. There was a crush behind her and, boxed in, unable to escape, she took the pen that Martha was offering her and bent over the form, keeping her head down as she slowly wrote a fresh bid.

Behind her someone began to complain that she was taking too long, dragging it out to stop anyone else bidding. As if...

She surrendered the pen, but her apology was brushed aside as the man pushed past her. Taking a swift step back, she caught her heel in her hem and, stumbling, flung out an arm, groping for something to grab onto and stop herself from falling. There was nothing, she was going down, but then, out of nowhere, a hand grasped hers, catching her, steadying her.

She didn't have to look to see who had saved her. It was a hand she knew. A callused hand that had scraped over sensitive skin, waking up hitherto unexperienced heights of pleasure and, for a few brief hours, blocking all pain.

For a heartbeat that hand was all that was

holding her up, but then a bell was rung for the end of the auction, jolting her back to reality and, as a cheer went up, she recovered her balance.

Keeping her head down, she muttered a hoarse, 'Thank you...'

No one heard. Kit had been enveloped in hugs, Martha was with friends and, finally, she was able to slip away.

Kit felt the woman's hand slip from his grasp in the crush but before he could go after her, make sure she was all right, he was being hugged by someone overjoyed at having made the winning bid for a trip.

He caught sight of her as she hurried away, presumably one of the unlucky ones who'd missed out at the last minute. Relieved that she was okay, he surrendered to the moment, congratulating the winners, all the while unable to shake the feeling that he'd seen something this evening, heard something. Missed something.

'Kit. It's good to see you, although not in these circumstances. How is your father?'

Martha Adams was one of his grandmother's oldest friends and he kissed her cheeks, introducing her to Lucy before answering her question.

'Frustrated. He's desperately trying to issue orders, but the words are eluding him.'

'The speech will come back, but it takes time. I imagine your mother has her hands full.'

'She's more than a match for him.'

'I'm glad to hear it. And how about you? How are you coping?'

'Brad is doing a great job and Laura is home, helping out. I'm trying to help but if I'm honest I'm just getting in everyone's way.' Getting in his brother's way. While he'd been chasing trophies, Brad had stepped into his shoes, buckling down to learn the business. Now his brother was convinced that Kit had returned to grab back his rightful place. 'Did you bid on anything tonight, ma'am?'

'I did,' she said. 'I'm going to your spa in Phuket and I couldn't be more excited. Have you been there?'

'I stopped over a couple of years ago when I was racing in that part of the world. It's beautiful and the staff are amazing. You'll have a wonderful time.'

* * *

Eve was sitting in the shadows on the terrace when Martha carefully lowered herself into the chair beside her with a contented sigh.

'I'm sorry to run out on you at the last moment, Martha,' she apologised. 'Did you win?'

'I did, thank you, but I saw that man push you out of the way. So rude. Are you all right?'

'The only harm was the hem of my dress and I'm sure you'd say that was a win. I just needed some fresh air.'

'Then you'd better take a big breath.' Martha handed her the folder she was holding. 'We're both going on a dream trip. You're going on safari.'

'What?' Eve's head was still reeling from the impact of the encounter with Kit. How close she'd come to being face-to-face with him and uncertain which would have been worse: the shock of recognition or the polite expression of a man who was being kind to a total stranger. 'No...' She was holding the glossy brochure, looking down at a photograph of the elephant and her baby. 'This can't be right. There was another bid. Right at the last moment...'

'The man who knocked you out of the way?

So rude. He dashed off a bid but I managed to top it in the last seconds before the bell rang.' She hesitated, for a moment uncertain. 'I saw the longing on your face when you were looking at that photograph, Eve. If I was wrong, I have no doubt that your rival bidder would be happy to pay the extra hundred dollars and take it off your hands.'

Overwhelmed with such a rush of conflicting emotions, at that moment Eve couldn't have said which way was up but there was one thing she was certain about.

'No.' Clutching the folder tightly to her chest, she said it again. 'No,' she repeated. 'I'm going home.' She looked at Martha. 'There's only one problem. You've volunteered Mary to look after Hannah, but who is going to look after the cat?'

Martha rolled her eyes. 'I fed Mungo until you arrived, I suppose I can do it again.'

'It's the annual audit next month, Brad. You have to be here for that,' Laura said. With their mother fully occupied looking after their father, it was just Kit, Brad and his sister Laura at the family meeting. 'I can go to Nymba for the trust meeting. It's just a formality, showing a Merchant face once a year.'

'It's not just a formality.' Brad's temper was wearing thin. 'The Nymba Trust are major partners. But even if it was, sending a nineteen-year-old student to represent the company might be seen as a touch too casual.'

'I'll go,' Kit said.

Brad threw his hands up in the air. 'Break out the spinach! It's Popeye the Sailor Man to the rescue.'

'It takes more than spinach to put a world-beating yacht in the water and win races,' Kit said, trying not to lose patience with his brother. He knew Brad had a lot on his plate. 'It takes teamwork, psychology and a great deal of diplomacy. This is me being diplomatic,' he added. 'You'll be a lot less stressed with me on a different continent.'

His brother's face twitched, but he was no-where near ready to take the olive branch.

'This isn't just swanning around, graciously showing your face once in a blue moon at one of the resorts so that a bit of the Kit Merchant glamour rubs off on the business. Nymba Lodge is a major partner, that's why Dad always goes himself.'

'Dad always went himself because he loves Africa. He treated it as a holiday,' his little pot-stirring sister said, getting her own back for the 'student' put-down. 'I'm sure Kit can handle that.'

'Undoubtedly. We all saw the pictures of him having a good time in the Med last year with that French guy and Matt Grainger—'

He broke off, as Kit stood.

The holiday he and Matt had spent in Nice with Philippe d'Usay had been the last occasion they'd all been together before the accident that had led to Matt's opiate addiction and death.

'That was the last good time Matt had anywhere,' he said.

The last good time he'd had anywhere.

'I'm sorry. I didn't mean—'

'Forget it.'

It sometimes felt as if Brad had arrived in the world resentful that he wasn't the first-born, but despite the fact that he sounded like a spoiled brat, and this time had strayed into dangerous territory, Kit had a certain amount of sympathy.

Guilt for not being there when Brad had needed him had never left him. Even when he could have come home and tried to mend fences with his father he'd made a conscious decision to give Brad a clear shot at succeeding their father as CEO.

His stroke should have been Brad's big moment to show the old man that he wasn't the second-best son. He was so wound up about it he'd convinced himself that his big brother—not content with gold-medal glory and a room full of trophies—had returned to steal his glory when nothing could be further from the truth.

His team were at the bottom of the world preparing for the biggest race in the yachting calendar and he should be with them.

He'd thought, once the crisis had passed, he would be able to make his peace and return to his team. Right now, with his father unable to talk in any way that was coherent, that was impossible, but it wouldn't hurt to start his peace initiative with his brother.

'Brad—'

Brad muttered something under his breath

but lifted a hand in surrender. 'Make sure you read the files before you go.'

'Can I ask one favour?'

'You want us to polish your trophies while you're away?'

He ignored the jibe. 'Lucy has been through a rough time. I thought she could do with a break, so I asked her to stay for the summer. She doesn't know anyone here, and with Mom busy looking after the old man, I thought maybe you could find something for her to do?'

'Don't worry, we'll look after her,' Laura said, quickly, before Brad compounded the insult by suggesting she polish them. 'Won't we, Brad?'

'Sure. Don't feel you have to rush back,' he added. 'We're used to managing without you.'

'Will you try and get it through his thick skull that I don't want his job?' Kit said when Brad had gone, then shook his head. 'Sorry, it's not your problem. This is my fault.'

Laura didn't argue with him, just said, 'I'll book your flight.'

'Thanks.'

'At least you'll have some home company while you're there. The woman who won the auction will be at Nymba at the same time. Genevieve Bliss. Did you meet her?'

'I imagine so. I made a point of thanking everyone. I'll be sure to say hello.'

CHAPTER THREE

NYMBA SAFARI LODGE was breathtaking. Eve's suite, sheltered from the sun by the canopy of the trees, had an open-air shower, a roll-top star bath and the four-poster bed, draped in gauzy netting, could be wheeled out onto the deck if she preferred to sleep outside.

Who wouldn't?

She'd broken her journey in London, spending a week sorting out her flat, but the second, even longer flight to Kabila had left her exhausted. She could have easily curled up and gone to sleep right there and then but she resisted the temptation.

This trip was the most unexpected, most self-indulgent of pilgrimages and she wasn't going to waste a minute of it.

Once her personal butler, Michael, had assured himself that she knew where everything was and how it worked and left her to settle in, she stripped off her travel-crumpled clothes. It felt slightly wicked to be naked out in the open air, but she was visible only to birds, curious monkeys, a giraffe standing on the far bank of the river and, relishing the sense of freedom, she stepped under the shower and washed the long journey from her hair and skin.

First warm and then wake-up-cold.

Refreshed, she wrapped herself in a bathrobe, filled a glass from the water cooler and leaned against the deck rail, just soaking in the view.

Nymba.

The name hadn't been a coincidence. This really was the site of her parents' *boma*. It was where, after a morning at the village school, under the eyes of a girl called Ketty, she had played, done her homework and taken care of the orphaned animals that had found a home with them.

The air was dry, warm, rich with the familiar scents of woodsmoke, wild basil, long hot days that baked the earth. Thrumming with the sound of cicadas.

A glossy starling landed on the deck rail, with a flash of metallic green wings, looking for crumbs, then took off as, high in the tree-tops, a monkey shrieked an alarm.

It was taken up by others along the riverbank and she leaned over the rail to see what had caused the fuss.

A family of elephants splashing and rolling in the mud took no notice, but the zebras and impalas, edgier and ever alert to danger, had lifted their heads to sniff the wind.

After a moment the noise began to die down and the animals lowered their heads to the water. If a predator had been slinking through the shadows, it had moved on. Maybe.

Out in the river, a hippo emerged just sufficiently to show the rounded half-hoop of her eyes. A family of warthogs, tails erect, trotted by and there were birds, too. Egrets, several different kinds of starlings and little yellow weaver birds busy at their nests filled the trees around her. Eve could have watched for hours, but she didn't have time to linger.

She had been given the itinerary at Reception and it was time to go down for afternoon tea before being taken on the evening game ride.

Her hair had dried so quickly into natural curls that it would need serious time with the straighteners before she could wind it into a chignon, but she'd been happy to leave them behind. The semi-permanent colour was fading out, too. In the bright sunlight she could see the glint of red shining through.

It didn't matter.

Kit Merchant was seven thousand miles away and, after a couple of weeks of only leaving the cottage to shop for groceries, she could relax.

She applied copious amounts of the body lotion that her mother had sworn was a better insect repellent than anything on the market, and factor fifty to any bit of skin that would be exposed. Her hair might be temporarily brown, but she had the skin of a redhead and she took the extra precaution of adding a heavy zinc sunblock to her nose and cheekbones before dressing in a pair of the khaki pants and long-sleeved shirt that had once belonged to her mother.

She had found them washed, neatly pressed and layered with lavender, along with her broad-brimmed hat and ankle boots, when she'd been clearing cupboards in the cottage. The discovery had provoked tears, but they were standard bush clobber with useful pockets and fitted as if they had been made for her.

Wearing them made her feel very close to her mother.

She swept her hair into a hairband, picked up her hat and headed across the walkway to the main building.

She'd already seen the thatched, open-sided central area where the reception and offices of the resort, along with a comfortable sitting area, were located.

The thatch extended over part of a stone terrace where tea was being served at a long table and a white-jacketed waiter drew back a seat for her.

She chose orange pekoe tea and, since the earlier arrivals were all staring at her, introduced herself.

'Hi, I'm Eve Bliss.'

They all responded with their names.

'You're American?' someone asked.

They were a mix of English, American and Japanese and in England everyone thought she was American. In America she easily slipped into her mother's New England accent but was often asked if she was English or Australian.

'My mother was American,' she said. She didn't talk about her English father, who had deserted them for a younger, less assertive assistant.

'And you speak the language,' someone else—Faye—said.

Was that why they were staring? Because she'd exchanged a few words with the waiter?

'It's not the local tribal language. Swahili is a lingua franca that's used all over east Africa. I picked it up when I lived here as a child. Have you been here long?' she asked. 'What have you seen?'

It was enough to turn the conversation away from her as they piled in with stories of their encounters with elephants, lions, a rare glimpse of a rhino. She listened with interest, making the appropriate noises as she tucked into the tiny sandwiches, scones and cakes that arrived on a tiered dish, along with a pot of tea.

Fortunately, she didn't have too much time to indulge her sweet tooth before they were collected for the evening game drive.

Eve didn't make it to dinner. Didn't see the stars from her sky bed or hear the cough of a lion. She didn't see or hear a thing until she opened her eyes to discover that the gauzy space she had fallen into was filled with a pearly pink predawn glow.

She lay there for a moment, putting together the where, the how…

Nymba. She was at Nymba and one sociable gin and tonic after the game drive had been enough for the jet lag she'd been fighting off all day to finally catch up with her.

She'd bailed on dinner—falling asleep with your face in your food was not a good look—and held herself together just long enough to tuck the mosquito netting around her bed before she closed her eyes and knew no more.

Right now she wanted nothing more than to take her time as the world awoke around her, but her itinerary started with an early morning river trip and she dragged her unwilling body under the shower. More or less awake, she tied back her still-damp hair and applied factor fifty to her skin and sunblock to her nose and cheekbones. Sunglasses usefully covered slightly puffy eyes and, hat in hand, she made her way along the treetop walk and down the steps to the terrace.

Breakfast wouldn't be served until after the early morning game viewing, but there was a buffet set up in the shade of the thatched roof, with pastries, juice, coffee and boiling water for tea.

She wasn't the only one desperate for a wake-up glass of orange juice. A man with the crumpled look of someone who had slept in his clothes drank down the glass he'd just poured and refilled it before realising there was someone behind him.

He turned, jug in hand, paused for a moment, no doubt startled by the picture she presented, before offering to fill the glass she'd picked up. 'Sorry, I'm hogging the juice...'

Eve felt the blood drain from her face.

It couldn't be.

Kit Merchant was supposed to be holding the fort in Nantucket.

Just as he'd been supposed to be aboard his yacht in the Southern Ocean.

Not.

As she hesitated, he gave her his full attention. 'Are you okay?'

Thanks to the sunglasses and thick white streaks of sunblock, he hadn't recognised her, which should have been off-the-scale okay, but she had the answer to the *Which would be worse?* question she'd asked herself back at the auction.

She knew it was wrong, that she should be relieved, glad even. To have him look at her the way he had that night... Well, that was the worst idea in the world.

He was waiting for an answer.

'Y...yes. Sorry. It's a bit early for the brain to be engaged.' She jammed her hat on her head, waiting for him to put down the jug and move away so that she could catch her breath. Fill her glass.

He hadn't recognised her. It was okay.

He wasn't ready to surrender the jug but turned to fill her glass. Unfortunately, her hand was shaking so much that he reached out to steady it.

His hand around hers did not help.

'Not to mention jet lag,' she added.

'Why don't you sit down?' he suggested. 'I'll bring this over for you.'

He didn't wait for a response, but deftly relieved her of the glass and led the way to a table set between two armchairs overlooking the river.

He set down her glass and, since her legs were not exactly cooperating, she sat down.

'Can I bring you anything else?' he asked.

No, no…

'I'm fine,' she said. And she would be. She just needed a minute for her heart to stop dancing a crazy tango, for her breathing to recover. She'd thought she was safe. Hadn't brought a top-up hair rinse with her—she'd planned to do that in London on the way back.

What on earth was he doing here? How long would he stay?

She was just congratulating herself that he hadn't joined her, was beginning to recover from the shock, when a waiter arrived with a tray containing two large cups of coffee, pastries, plates and napkins.

'Have you got everything you need?' Kit asked, as he sank into the chair beside her.

Eve unglued her tongue from the roof of her mouth. 'Rather more than I can manage in five minutes.'

'Five minutes?'

'I have a canoe waiting.' Escape for a couple of hours while she figured out what she was going to do.

'That explains the warpaint,' he said and, just as he had once before, extended his hand and said, 'Kit Merchant.'

She'd had her minute. It wasn't nearly enough...

With no choice but to take it, she responded with what she hoped was the firm grasp of a woman in control of her limbs, if nothing else. 'Genevieve Bliss. Eve,' she added.

'Our very generous auction bidder. Laura asked me to look out for you.' He frowned. 'Why didn't we meet that night? I thought I'd thanked all the winning bidders personally and I wouldn't have forgotten you.'

Which had to be the very definition of irony...

'I tripped over the hem of my dress,' she said. 'You might remember catching me.'

'That was you? You rushed away before I could make sure you were all right.'

He was still holding her hand and she forced herself to let go and reach for her juice.

'I thought I'd been beaten at the last moment,' she said, hoping that the glass wouldn't rattle against her teeth as she took a sip.

'I hope you're glad that you won. Despite the jet lag,' he added, when she didn't immediately answer. 'That is one seriously tough journey.'

'It helps if you stay over in London for a day or two.'

'Is that what you did?' Kit reached for his coffee. 'I'm catching a touch of British in your accent.'

He'd said that, too. That night…

'I've been working there,' she said, without confirming her nationality one way or the other. 'I took a journey break to sort out a few things.'

A friend had suggested putting her flat on a rental site since she was going to be away longer than expected.

'Lucky you. This is a business trip and I didn't have time to indulge my love of London.'

Her stopover had mostly involved cleaning and packing away stuff to leave wardrobe and cupboard space free, arranging for a cleaner to come in between visitors, but she murmured her sympathy.

Kit rested his head against the back of the chair. 'This is so peaceful.'

If she'd thought about it, she would have assumed that the Merchant family were closely acquainted with all their resorts, but Kit hadn't been part of the business. 'You haven't been here before?'

The corner of his mouth lifted in a self-mocking smile. 'It's landlocked.'

He was inviting her to laugh at him, or maybe with him, it was hard to tell.

'There's a river,' she ventured.

'Are you suggesting I join you on your canoe trip?'

'N-no.' The last thing she wanted was for him to think she was flirting with him. 'I'm sure it's full.' But he looked exhausted. He had looked tired at the auction... 'Maybe you could go this evening. We all need to slow down once in a while.'

He followed her gaze to look out across the still calm of the oxbow lake, reflecting the pink sky, but she suspected his thoughts were on a distant sea.

'How is your father?' she asked.

He came back from wherever he had been, lifted a shoulder. 'Stubborn, difficult, opinion-ated.'

'Getting better, then.'

The smile returned, this time deeper, provoking memories that she'd tried very hard to forget.

'He's recovering, but he's going to have to change his diet, take more exercise, avoid stress. My mother is going to be very busy.'

'And happy to be so, I'm sure.'

Martha had been full of the Merchants on the way home from the auction; they were one of those couples who had fallen in love in high school and never looked at another person.

'Yes,' he said. 'It's the kind of marriage you don't often see.' He glanced across at her. 'The kind built on friendship and respect, that is strong enough to endure the rough times. The kind that you hope for.'

CHAPTER FOUR

KIT, TALKING ABOUT his parents' love for one another, had spoken from the heart and Eve had to swallow down a large lump in her throat.

'I hope you find that for yourself,' she said, trying not to think about his tenderness towards Lucy. They had worked together, had an enduring bond in their love of sailing, of her brother, something solid on which to build a future...

A single night of passion, no matter how life-changing the result, was not a basis for any kind of relationship. In the lonely dark she might have longed for the touch of a man who had, no matter how briefly, lifted her heart, made her laugh, made her body sing, but with the dawn came reality...

Sitting beside him in the golden heat of an African dawn was something else entirely.

'How long do you think it will be before you can return to racing?' she asked.

Not an entirely disinterested question.

'It may never happen.'

'I'm sorry.' That wasn't a selfish 'sorry'. Sailing was his life. 'This must be so hard for you.'

He glanced at her. 'I've had a good run and now I'm needed at home. Needed here...'

'Is there a problem?' She shook her head. 'Sorry, it's none of my business.'

They were a couple of strangers having a polite conversation and if her pulse rate was unnaturally fast, she'd got over it once and would again.

If there was a problem, he'd be locked away with the staff while he was here and, needed at home, on his way in twenty-four or, at the most, forty-eight hours.

She just needed to keep her head down and her hat on in the meantime.

Kit leaned forward, picked up the plate of pastries and offered them to her. 'You should eat something, Eve. Breakfast is the most important meal of the day.'

She'd been struggling to lose the last of the weight that had clung on after she'd given birth to Hannah, finished breastfeeding, but her stomach gave a little gurgle of excitement at the sight of an almond croissant.

He heard and grinned. Blushing with embarrassment, she said, 'I missed dinner last night.'

'Then I must insist, in the cause of health and safety, that you eat something before you face the wildlife.'

Once it had become obvious that he didn't recognise her, she'd begun to relax a little. They had met as strangers and yet right from the first moment the connection had been so intense, so immediate. And it was still there.

While they'd been talking the rest of the guests had gathered, quickly downing juice, coffee and grabbing a pastry. Now they were beginning to disperse on their chosen method of game watching and it was time for her to move, too.

'If I don't go now my canoe will leave without me,' she said, 'but I'll take this to keep me going.' She picked up the croissant, biting into it as she forced herself to her feet, forced herself to walk away.

'Watch out for the crocodiles,' he said, rising with her, in an instinctive gesture of courtesy.

'It's a little-known fact,' she told him, gathering the pastry flakes from her lips and sucking them from her finger as she took a step back, 'that more people are killed by hippos than crocs.'

'Really. And you're going out there in a canoe?'

'It was on the itinerary I was given when I arrived. I've no doubt they would have changed it if I'd asked, but it's unbelievably peaceful on the water.'

'Peace and quiet sounds rather wonderful just now. Are you sure there isn't room on your canoe for a late arrival?'

Laughter reached them from the compound where guests were piling into the large four-by-four game-viewing vehicles. Relaxed, having fun, their only concern whether they had their cameras fully charged...

Kit had arrived tired and irritated, certain, with time to reflect on the long flight, that his brother had played him. The last thing Brad wanted was a reconciliation between Kit and their father and he'd used this meeting as a means of getting him out of the way.

He rubbed a hand over his face in an attempt to wake himself up, focus on why he was here, but it had been a bad few weeks and he felt drawn to the peace and quiet of Eve's canoe.

Or maybe it was just Eve.

She had taken a step back, distancing herself from him at his suggestion that he accompany her in the canoe. Not exactly a textbook reaction to an invitation from him. But then his invitations had always been rare; he was always the one creating the distance, but as Eve's tongue swept a stray crumb from her lower lip a kick of heat shot through him and he put the plate down before the rest of the pastries hit the floor.

'Jet lag,' she warned, and he would have been hard put to say whether it was sympathy or relief that he heard in her voice. 'Give breakfast a miss and take a nap.'

'Do I look that bad?' he asked.

'*Memsahib...*'

She said something in Swahili to the man waiting to escort her to her canoe before saying, 'You look exhausted. It will catch up with you sooner rather than later. Far better to be lying down when it does.'

She took another step back and, with a nod, turned to follow the man across the terrace, only hesitating when she reached the steps that led down to the dock to glance back. Almost, he thought, as if she regretted her decision.

Her face was shadowed by the brim of her hat and he wished he could see her eyes.

She'd chatted, been interested, thoughtful and yet he couldn't get a grip of what she was actually thinking. Whether she was just being charming to some poor bloke who looked like hell after travelling for twenty-four hours or... Or nothing.

He took a mental step back of his own.

Eve Bliss was wearing clothes chosen for comfort rather than style. Her hair, bundled up off her face, was mostly hidden beneath her hat, apart from a few wisps that had escaped. And she'd hidden her eyes, most of her face masked by a pair of large dark glasses and the white streaks of sunblock.

Pretty much all he could see of her had been her mouth, which would explain why it had been the sole focus of his attention from the moment she bit into that pastry. And yet that little lick of an admittedly luscious lip, the defensive lift of her chin, had tugged at some elusive memory.

It had been there from the moment he'd turned and seen her standing behind him. Nothing he could pin down. Nothing, despite the promise of a luscious body beneath the khaki clothes, and an intriguingly familiar accent, to have him thinking to hell with the jet lag, I want more of this, and following her to the canoe.

It had been there at the auction, too. Their only connection had been when he'd stopped her from falling, a quick glimpse of a very ordinary shade of brown hair, a plain black dress. He should be surprised that he remembered that much and yet, as he'd watched her hurry away, he'd felt what he could only describe as a disturbance in the atmosphere and later, as he'd rubbed the exhaustion from his face, there had been the scent of vanilla...

He shook his head. This was crazy.

He'd been tired that night. Even under stress he could sleep on a clothesline—it went with the job—but he'd been feeling guilty about Brad, who wanted this so much. Guilty about not wanting this when it meant so much to his father. Guilty about leaving his team at such a critical moment.

Everyone had been sympathetic to hear about

the old man's stroke, but they'd expected Kit back within a week, two at the most.

Not one of them would understand why he'd apparently abandoned them at such a critical moment.

It hadn't taken the furious response from the sponsors to his resignation as skipper for him to understand that walking away at such a vital moment could well be the end of his career as an international yachtsman. But he'd made a promise, even though his father hadn't been listening, had turned his back, waved him away, that if, when, he was needed, he would be there.

He rubbed his hands briskly over his face, attempting to get his head in gear, trying to figure out what he was missing and there it was again.

Vanilla...

Who was she?

Eve's east coast accent was subtly layered with the kind of British accent spoken by women who hung around the yachting crowd. She'd said she worked in London, but she wasn't sharply enough turned out to be with one of the PR teams or the gossip media that hung around the yachts hoping for photographs or stories.

Even on safari they wouldn't have been seen dead in a khaki shirt and pants with the washed-out look of long use that contrasted so starkly with the brand-new gear worn by the rest of the visitors.

They looked like tourists. She didn't.

Unlike the other guests, who had now dispersed on their game rides, hot-air-balloon trips, or whatever else was on offer, she seemed part of this place. She spoke the language, for heaven's sake. The staff had spoken to her in Swahili and she'd replied. Not just the standard 'hello' and 'thank you' that everyone picked up but in whole sentences.

He shook his head, dismissing the feeling that they had, somehow, met before. That couldn't be true; he knew to his cost that the slightest acquaintance was enough to have women clinging to him.

It wasn't vanity, it wasn't even about him; anyone with cover appeal would do and he had learned to avoid the worst of it.

The sponsors, however, wanted their money's worth.

Their yacht, their name, on front covers of the glossies and it was the PR team's job to make sure it got there. They threw the models and actresses in his direction and he was expected to catch them. His only memory of the occasion would be the sight of a magazine cover as he passed through an airport.

Eve, he thought, despite her understated wardrobe, wasn't a woman you'd forget.

'Mr Merchant, can I show you to your suite?'

He'd dumped his bag at Reception, desperate for coffee and to arrange to meet the Merchant partners so that he could leave as soon as possible, but Eve was right.

He'd been travelling for more than twenty-four hours, was seven hours out of his time zone and he needed to at least take a shower before he met with anyone vital to the smooth running of their partnership.

Kit listened patiently while Patrick, his butler, gave him a tour of the suite, then said, 'Miss Bliss bid on a charity auction for her stay here. I hope she's being given the VIP treatment?'

'Yes, sir. As soon as our receptionist saw her name on the guest list she allocated her our very best suite.' He indicated a sky suite a little ahead of him to the right and just visible through the trees.

'Her name? You know her? She's a regular visitor?'

'No, sir. This is her very first visit to the Nymba Safari Lodge, but our receptionist, Ketty Ngei, knew her when she was a little girl and lived here with her parents. She was very much looking forward to greeting her, but her grandfather had to go to the hospital and she has accompanied him to the city.'

She'd lived here? Well, that explained a lot.

'Ketty Ngei? Is she related to Joshua Ngei?' He was the village elder who'd signed the original partnership agreement with his father. The man he'd come to meet.

'Mzee Ngei is her grandfather,' Patrick confirmed.

'Is he ill?'

'I'm sorry, sir, I couldn't say. Is there anything else I can bring you?'

'No, thank you.'

He set an alarm on his watch for lunchtime before he stripped off, took a shower and lay down under the cool of a stunningly wrought thatched roof. Would it be possible to have something like it on his beach cabin on Nantucket? They used thatch in England, but would it stand up to Atlantic gales?

His last thought, before sleep claimed him, was the memory of an extraordinary night he'd once spent there with an English girl who, like Cinderella, had vanished without trace, leaving behind not a glass slipper but a beloved grey velvet elephant to prove that it hadn't all been a dream.

Apart from the initial wobble with the glass, Eve thought she'd handled her unexpected encounter with Kit Merchant pretty well, all things considered.

In some ways it had been made easy for her. He knew that she'd been at the auction, so he expected her to know who he was and that he'd come home because his father was ill.

She'd even handled the suggestion that he might join her in the canoe without choking on her croissant.

But when she'd risked a glance back, she'd discovered that he was watching her. Had some small gesture, the way she moved her head, her mixed-up accent, triggered a memory, waking a synapse that was flickering but not quite making the connection? Like an old neon sign that was struggling to light.

She was the only one heading down to the waiting canoe and it would have been so easy to call out to him.

She would have insisted that he sit in front and then spent the entire trip looking at his wide shoulders, the lick of sun-bleached hair that settled in the nape of his neck, knowing exactly where he had a tattoo of a famous cartoon sailor and how his skin had tasted as she'd kissed it…

Her skin heated at the thought and a low ache settled in her womb as she closed her eyes, for a moment succumbing to the memory.

Madness…

Her breathing went to pot and she had to grip hold of her seat to stop her hands from shaking.

'You will be safe.' The man guiding the canoe through the water, no doubt putting her nerves down to the sight of crocodiles basking on the far bank, attempted to reassure her.

'Yes. I know how skilled you are,' she replied before realising that the man had spoken to her not in Swahili but in the local dialect. And she had answered in the same language.

She turned in her seat to look at him and he grinned.

'Hello, Evie,' he said, in English. 'Long time, no see.'

She took off her dark glasses. 'Peter? Peter Ngei?' He'd been several years older than her and there had been a huge party before he'd left to study law at the same time as she'd been sent off to boarding school. 'Mom wrote to tell me that you'd got a first. What on earth are you doing paddling a tourist canoe? You should be a judge by now.'

He laughed. 'I'm getting there, but I was at home when Ketty told us you were coming to Nymba, so I volunteered to pick you up and bring you to the village. Unless you're only interested in the hippos? Maybe you're too grand for us now?'

'You have got to be kidding! My grandmother left me some money or I'd never have been able to afford this trip.'

'I'm sorry to hear that you have lost her. And your dear mother. The village wept when we received her bequest for equipment, books, for the school. Mzee Ngei put up a plaque in her honour.'

'She left money for the school?'

'You didn't know?'

She shook her head.

Her mother had made a number of charitable bequests, but she hadn't been able to stay in the room while the will was read.

It had been worth this trip just to hear that.

She blinked away the stinging sensation at the back of her eyes and said, 'So tell me about you, Peter. What are you doing? Are you married?'

'I'm in the Attorney General's office, married to Maria and we have two boys.'

'Maria…?'

'It was always Maria,' he said.

'Of course it was.' They were another couple of childhood sweethearts… 'I'm so happy for you. Is she here?'

'No, she's working and the boys are in school, but it's Mzee's birthday next weekend and she's bringing the boys down for the party. What about you, Evie?'

'Nothing so grand. I'm an out-of-work teacher, not married,' she replied, 'with one little girl.'

'You didn't bring her with you?'

'She was three in May. Most safari lodges don't take children younger than six and Nymba doesn't take them at all.'

'Next time, come and stay in the village,' he said, neatly edging the canoe alongside a jetty. 'We take children of any age.'

As if to emphasise that fact, a dozen or more children ran down to meet them before stopping abruptly to stare at her as she stepped from the canoe.

'My grandmother has told them that your hair is redder than the setting sun,' Peter said. 'They can't wait to see it.'

'Oh, dear.'

'Problem?'

'For reasons far too complicated to go into, it's now a rather boring shade of brown.' She looked at the children. 'Maybe a picture of Hannah will do the job.'

She opened her bag and took out a leather folder, which contained photographs of her daughter. She took one out, folded herself up so that she was on their level, and held it up for them to see.

There was a collective gasp and when one,

braver than the rest, came closer to look, Eve handed it to her to pass around.

'You may have lost that,' Peter warned.

'I am a besotted mother. I never travel with less than six photographs of my baby. Plus the ones on my phone.'

She offered him the folder and he smiled. 'She is beautiful. The image of you as a child. Almost. I assume she got the blue eyes from her father. He's not with you?'

She barely hesitated before shaking her head. 'We are not together.' She raised an eyebrow. 'I've shown you mine...?' she prompted, to divert him.

He produced a phone and brought up pictures of the cheekiest-looking little boys.

'Oh, they are gorgeous, Peter.'

'They are a handful...' That was as far as he got before she was engulfed in hugs.

Kit was standing under a cold shower. He'd been dreaming. It was one of those recurring dreams that haunted you, where you were looking for someone, travelling down endless corridors until you woke in a sweat.

It hadn't happened in a while but, considering

the way his life had been turned upside down, his disturbed sleep pattern, the fact that he'd been thinking about Red as he fell asleep, it wasn't surprising.

The sun was high now. Across the river, the savannah shimmered in a heat haze so that at one moment you were looking at a distant herd of zebra and the next they had vanished.

He raised the canvas sidings to let the air blow through and found himself looking into the huge, long-lashed eyes of a giraffe.

They stared at one another for a hold-your-breath moment and then the creature blinked and moved gracefully away to continue grazing on the trees.

A bird swooped past, a flash of blue and mauve, and as he followed it he found himself looking into the face of a small monkey. It bared its teeth at him, swung down on the rail beside him, leapt across the deck and grabbed an orange from a bowl of fruit.

And Kit laughed.

For the first time in weeks, he threw back his head and laughed. Eve would be back from her canoe trip and he couldn't wait to tell her.

She'd probably roll her eyes, tell him that it

happened all the time, but he didn't care. She could roll her eyes all she wanted so long as she sat next to him at lunch and he could catch her scent.

CHAPTER FIVE

LUNCH WAS BEING served when he reached the terrace, but a glance along the table was enough for him to see that Eve was not there.

Disappointed and a little concerned, he crossed to Reception.

'Has Miss Bliss returned from her canoe trip?' he asked.

'No, sir, she won't be back until this evening. She is spending the day with friends in the village.'

She hadn't mentioned that when she was telling him how peaceful and quiet it would be on the river. No wonder she hadn't wanted company.

'Mr Lenku wondered if you would prefer to eat in the privacy of the staff dining room, sir?'

He nodded. 'Yes, thank you. Would you ask him to join me?'

He was here for a meeting, not to indulge his curiosity, indulge anything over a woman.

He'd met James Lenku briefly on his arrival. He was an experienced resort manager, and Kit was relying on him for a briefing before the meeting the next day.

'What time will it start?' he asked, when James arrived.

'I've just heard that the meeting will have to be put back for two or three days, Mr Merchant—'

'Kit.'

He nodded. 'Kit. Mzee Ngei had a hospital appointment today and they have decided to keep him there for some tests. His grandson, Peter Ngei, is now in control of the day-to-day running of the trust, but the annual meeting can't go ahead without Mzee present. Your father usually stayed for a week,' he added, 'so there is no problem over your accommodation.'

What had been Brad's parting shot? Don't hurry back...

'Is there anything we can do to make Mr... Mzee Ngei's stay more comfortable?'

'Ketty will take care of anything he needs. She'll let me know if she needs anything.'

'Do we have any idea how long it's likely to be? As you know my father is not well and I'm needed at home.'

'Not long. It's his birthday on Saturday and the village are throwing a big party. Nothing will keep him from that and in the meantime you have an opportunity to experience what Nymba Lodge has to offer the guests you send to us.'

He'd thought he was going to be doing something useful, but apparently this annual meeting was going to be more of a holiday, as it had been a holiday for his father, and he had to fill his time.

'Certainly. What would you suggest?'

'There are regular hot-air-balloon flights, river trips, fishing and walking with the elephants.'

'Walking with them? I thought African elephants were invariably dangerous.'

'These were orphans raised at Nymba by the behavioural biologist team who worked here. Rose and Jeremy Bliss. I believe you know Eve Bliss, their daughter?'

'We have met,' he confirmed. 'Were the elephants part of their work?'

'They were here studying the local population. I believe they rescued the babies after their mothers were killed by poachers. The trust has taken care of them since the project ended.'

'Will Eve be going on the walk?'

'I can check her itinerary and arrange for you to be in her party.'

That wasn't what he'd asked... Except why else would he have asked? 'Thank you.'

They paused while lunch was served and then Kit asked, 'What is likely to be raised at the meeting? It seems to be little more of an annual formality, but are you aware of any problems that might come up?'

'The relationship between the trust and Merchant is not something I'm involved in,' he said. 'Peter Ngei is the man you need to talk to. He'll be bringing Miss Bliss back to the lodge this evening. I'll send a message to ask if he can spare you some time then.'

Later, having checked the time difference to make sure that the Nantucket office would be open, he called to update Brad on the delay. Not that it would bother him. His sister answered.

'Hi, Kit, how was the flight?'

'Long. How's Dad?'

'Getting grouchier with every passing day, which I take to be a good sign. How's Africa?'

'So far I've had a face-to-face with a giraffe, a monkey stole an orange from my fruit bowl and the meeting with the trust is delayed because the main player is in hospital.'

'What can I say? Sit back and enjoy the view.'

'I have it covered. I do have a preliminary meeting with the guy who actually runs the Nymba Trust this evening. Can Brad spare a moment? If he's not too busy polishing my trophies.'

'He's not too busy with anything. He's taken Lucy over to the boathouse.'

'The boathouse? We are talking about Brad Merchant?'

'You asked us to look after her, so he took her to a Chamber of Commerce dinner last night.'

'Poor woman. I hope the food was good.'

'It's only around you that he's a grouch, Kit. Most of the time he's quite likeable. For a brother,' she added, pointedly. 'Anyway, they must have done more than eat because this morning, he was all about her starting a sailing class for the younger kids.'

'I'm speechless.'

'Always the perfect response.'

'Come on, Laura, we both know that Brad

hasn't been near the boathouse since London,' he said.

'It's difficult having to live with always being second best, Kit. His way of handling it was not to compete. He turned to the business because it was something you didn't care about.'

And now he was back getting in his brother's way.

'He loved sailing, Laura. I should have been a better brother, been there when he needed me, when you both needed me.'

When Matt had needed him.

'You can't change the past, Kit. You have to live with it and move on. Have you called Lucy?' she asked.

'I called her when I had a layover in London and texted her when I arrived. I'll call her now.'

'Don't trouble yourself. Brad is doing a good job.'

'Brad... She's fragile, Laura. If Brad is making a play for her because he thinks it will hurt me...'

'You'll probably be surprised to hear this, Kit, but it's not all about you. Life doesn't stop when you're not around. Quite the contrary.'

'Laura—'

'How's our auction winner?' she said, abruptly changing the subject. 'Have you met her?'

His sister didn't give off the same hostile vibes as his brother, but she had blamed him for not being there when he was needed. He'd let them both down, but their feelings had been lost in the row with his father...

'Eve? Yes, I bumped into her at some unearthly hour this morning when she was going on a canoe trip.'

'Did she have a good time?'

'I don't know.'

'Maybe you'd better brush up on that diplomacy you were telling us about. I'll ask Brad to call you,' she said and cut the connection.

He stared at the phone in his hand for a long moment. It wasn't just with his father that he needed to build bridges. He was in need of a major construction programme.

He called his mother, who was kinder and reassured him that his father was 'progressing'. His call to Lucy went to voicemail—all he could do was leave a message to let her know that he was thinking of her. That she was loved.

* * *

'Thank you so much for a lovely day, Peter,' Eve said. 'It was a joy to meet everyone and catch up with all the news.'

The canoe had been ferried back to the lodge earlier and she had expected him to turn around after dropping her off but, having helped her down from the four-by-four, he escorted her into the lodge.

'Christopher Merchant sent a message asking if I could spare him a few minutes,' he explained. 'He's here for the Merchant annual meeting with the Nymba Trust.'

Christopher... She had never heard him called that but, of course, he must have been named for his father.

'That sounds serious.'

Of course it was serious. Kit wouldn't have flown out here in the middle of a family crisis to count the spoons. He had a lot more on his mind than a long-ago night spent with some girl who wouldn't even tell him her name.

Peter just smiled. 'I'll text you about the school project and the party, but you're welcome at any time.'

Peter kissed her cheeks, they exchanged a hug

and, leaving him to his meeting, she headed across the lounge towards her suite.

'Hello, Eve.'

She jumped at the sound of Kit's voice. He'd been sitting, half hidden in a corner, and as she turned the light from his laptop threw his face into shadows, giving him an almost sinister look.

'I'm glad to see you've returned safely,' he said, rising to his feet. 'When you didn't come back this morning, I was sure a croc must have got you.'

Her morning disguise was gone. The zinc stripes had long since worn off her nose and cheekbones. She'd given her hairband to a child, her hat was in her hand and, with the sun dropping below the horizon, she'd propped her dark glasses on top of her head.

He was now looking straight into her eyes and she felt naked.

'Kit... As you see, I'm still in one piece.'

'I was all set to send out a search party,' he said, 'but James told me that you were having lunch with friends in the village.'

He'd actually checked?

'It was a totally unexpected treat. Peter took me completely by surprise this morning.'

'Peter?'

Kit was regarding her through narrowed eyes and, feeling utterly exposed, she turned to introduce them. 'Peter, may I introduce Kit Merchant? Kit, Peter Ngei.' Then, using her hat as a fan to hide her face, she said, 'If you'll excuse me, gentlemen, I'll leave you to your meeting.'

Kit took a step after her. This morning Eve's sunglasses had hidden her eyes. Green eyes, flecked with amber. Eyes that had haunted him for nearly four years.

'Mr Merchant?'

Red? Eve Bliss was Red? His boyishly slender Cinderella?

Even as he thought it, doubt set in. Eve's figure had a ripeness to it, her hair was the wrong colour. Could she be an older sister—?

'Where is Christopher Merchant?' Peter Ngei demanded.

'I'm Christopher Merchant,' he snapped, not looking around, but continuing to stare after Eve.

'But not the one I was expecting to meet.'

What?

'I'm sorry,' he said, apologising for his lack of attention. 'It was a long flight and my head feels as if it's still somewhere over the Sahara. I'm Christopher Merchant III,' he said, trying to put what he thought he'd seen out of his mind and focus on why he was here. 'My father is recovering from a stroke. It's going to take a while so I'm standing in for him. Everyone calls me Kit.'

The man gave him a long thoughtful look, glanced in the direction that Eve had taken and then back at him.

'I'm not everyone, Mr Merchant,' he replied, pointedly ignoring his outstretched hand.

Not a great start. Peter Ngei already thought he was dealing with the second team and his moment of inattention hadn't improved the situation.

It didn't help that, having seen the man hugging Eve, he wanted to punch him in the face.

Eve had to be Red.

You didn't feel that kind of intensity about someone with whom you'd spent no more than five minutes. Even this morning, behind dark

glasses, the sunblock, the hat, he'd felt the connection.

He'd wrapped those wild curls around his
fingers, looked into her eyes when the pupils
were dilated with desire, knew that mouth and
body intimately...

The moment he'd first set eyes on her that
night on the beach, even before her hand had
come into his, he'd recognised a life-changing
moment.

He'd called her Red and she'd blazed into
his life for one night, giving him everything
and more. And then she'd vanished, not on
the stroke of midnight, but just as effectively,
leaving him with nothing but a toy elephant to
prove that he hadn't dreamed the whole thing.

His sister, a self-absorbed teen besotted with
the boy she was with that night, hadn't noticed
her at the beach party, had no idea who she was
or who she might have come with.

He'd roamed the island on his bike, the elephant in his backpack, hoping to catch a glimpse
of flame-red hair until he'd left for France to
prepare for the round-the-world yacht race.

'Mr Ngei. I didn't realise you'd arrived.'
James emerged from the office in a flurry of

concern. 'I see you have already met Mr Merchant. Shall we go through to the office? Kit?' he prompted.

Kit dragged his mind out of the past. He was here to represent his family and, so far, wasn't doing a great job.

Eve showered, washing off the dust of the day, wrapped herself in a towelling robe and took her laptop out to the deck. She talked to Hannah about her day, checked in with Martha to make sure she was coping with the cat and then found herself typing Kit's name into the search engine.

There were dozens of pictures of him at the helm of terrifying yachts, with trophies, with girls, but the most recent were of him at the funeral of his friend Matt Grainger. In all of them, he was with Lucy, his arm around her, supporting her. In one she had turned to sob into his shoulder and he was holding her as if he would never let her go...

She closed the laptop, put it down. While she'd been surfing, the sky had darkened to black, the stars had turned on their light show and the moon was rising, huge and white, silvering the landscape.

Below her, along the river, frogs began their nightly chorus. There were discrete splashes and plops as hippos emerged, the cries of nightjars, rustles through the treetops as small night creatures hunted for insects. The slightly disturbing sound of an infant crying that was made by a bushbaby.

All alien to anyone who lived in a city, or on an island off the east coast of the US, and yet, to her, so familiar...

There was a gentle tap on the gate to her suite and for a moment her heart stopped.

She couldn't be certain that Kit had recognised her, but there had been a reaction in that moment when, stripped of her mask, she had come face-to-face with him. Not so much recognition as confusion.

Peter's presence, their meeting, meant that he hadn't been able to do anything, say anything, ask the question, but she had been sitting in the African night, waiting for him to come.

Or not. She hadn't claimed a previous acquaintance and he had Lucy in his life now. Maybe he'd just leave it.

But if he did come?

She'd been sitting in the dark imagining what he'd say to her. What she'd say to him if he came, if he called her Red.

Just dismiss that night as a bit of fun, nothing to fuss about? He hadn't recognised her, and she hadn't wanted to embarrass him. Cue a few awkward moments, careful avoidance of one another until he left in a day or two. But then they'd both be in Nantucket, living in the same small town. They couldn't avoid one another for ever and it wasn't just her. One look at Hannah and he'd know...

Kit Merchant was Hannah's father. Hannah had a right to know who she was. Kit had the right to know that he had a daughter, to decide if he wanted to be a father.

It might be easier for her if he said thanks, but no thanks. Her father had never been interested in her or his grandchild. But it was Kit's choice to make, not hers.

'Memsahib?'

Her body sagged. It wasn't Kit at her gate. It was Michael.

'You missed dinner, Miss Eve. We wondered if you were too tired to come down. Or not feeling well. Is there something I can bring you?'

'I'm perfectly well, Michael. I had a rather large lunch at the village but thank you for your concern.'

'It is a long time until morning. I could bring something to put in your fridge in case you become hungry in the night?'

'Nothing to eat, but perhaps some tea?' she suggested. 'Camomile?'

'Shall I light the lamps for you?'

She shook her head. 'We never see this kind of dark in London, Michael. Never see stars so thick and bright.' So close that you could almost touch them.

Kit tapped on the gate that led to Eve's suite and, at her invitation to come in, crossed the deck and placed the tray on the table beside her.

'Is the resort so short of staff that they have had to draft in management for room service?' she asked, without turning around.

The lack of surprise, almost as if she'd been

expecting him, the slight, almost undetectable shake in her voice was enough to confirm what he already knew.

Where to take it from here was something else.

Every instinct was to reach out, take her hand, just say, 'Hi, Red. I've been looking for you. I've missed you...' but he'd had a lot of time to think about how it would go if he ever found her.

To think about every second from the moment he'd seen her sitting on her own, the setting sun turning her hair into a fiery halo of curls.

She hadn't just distanced herself bodily from the party. She'd had the lost, slightly melancholy look of someone whose head was somewhere else and that would have taken him to her side even if she hadn't been strikingly beautiful.

In the cold light of day, faced with the reality of an empty cabin with not so much as a note with a phone number or pointed comment on his disappearance, the fact that she hadn't told him her name, it had seemed unlikely that there was no one in her life.

He'd kept his search low-key, afraid that what had happened between them had been a reaction to a row with a lover, partner, husband even and that, with daylight, she'd regretted her recklessness.

Were they still together?

She'd been at the auction, but it was obvious now that she'd avoided him so presumably had not been on her own.

She was alone here, however, and not wearing a ring of any kind, but had still acted as if they had never met when she'd seen him this morning, and again this evening. Maybe her response to the fact that he hadn't recognised her, but she could hardly blame him for that. She'd changed her hair colour and been covered up so completely that she could have been wearing a disguise.

Until he knew more, he would be content to have finally found her, to have a second chance of getting to know her, and leave it to her to decide when—if—she chose to acknowledge the night they had spent together.

'You have your eyes closed, Eve,' he said, putting the tray down on the table beside her. 'How did you know that I wasn't Michael?'

'He has a heavier footstep.'

'Then the next question has to be how did you know it was me?'

A little sigh escaped her. 'You bring an unexpected scent of the sea to the hot African dust.'

'The sea?' And this time it was his voice that was not quite steady. There was intimacy to scent. It involved touch, taste... For an age after they had made love, the scent of vanilla had clung to him. It had drawn him to bakeries. He had smelt it on his hands after the auction and he could smell it now. 'The nearest ocean has to be five hundred miles east.'

'Nearer seven hundred.' She opened her eyes and looked up at him. 'Maybe you have spent so much time being swept by saltwater spray that it has permeated your skin. Become a part of you.'

Now, he thought, she was going to say it now, but when the silence continued, he said, 'I waylaid Michael with your tray because I hoped you might spare me a little of your time.'

She glanced at the table. 'Really? Did you send him back for the pot of coffee? Not a good choice this late in the evening unless you're planning to stay up all night in the hope of seeing a leopard.'

'Is that likely?'

'The game wardens bait a tree on the other side of the river. Sit quietly and you may be lucky.'

There was the faint creak as, taking that as an invitation, he lowered himself into the cane armchair on the far side of the table.

'Can I pour your tea?' he asked.

'Michael would have added a Miss Eve to that.'

He began to relax.

He'd once, desperate to please, taken a girl to see some historical chick flick. At one point a pair of illicit lovers had met at a masked ball, pretending not to know one another, hiding their flirtation in full sight as they had danced together. He'd been fifteen, bored out of his mind, but he finally got the point of that scene.

Fifteen, he realised, knew nothing.

'You expect me to play butler?' he asked, managing to sound just a touch affronted.

'You brought the tray, you're about to pour the tea,' she pointed out.

The only light came from the soft glow of

solar-powered lights around the edge of the deck, but the moon was full and huge, silvering her cheeks, creating a wild silhouette of curls that, in his head, was that extraordinary clear, bright red.

It had been weeks since he'd felt like smiling but he did his best to keep it out of his voice as he said, 'Would you care for honey with your tea, Miss Eve?'

'Yes, please. Just one spoonful.'

He added the honey, handed her the cup and then, done with butlering, picked up his coffee and leaned back in his chair.

Eve hadn't asked why he was here, which suggested she knew, but there was no rush.

This was a good moment and he didn't want to spoil it by saying something stupid.

CHAPTER SIX

EVE STIRRED HER TEA, not at all sure what to make of this turn of events.

The last few moments had felt very much like flirting. In the darkness, the intimacy of the moment, she could imagine spilling out the truth and that, somehow, it would all be okay.

She glanced across at Kit. The shadows threw his face in contrast, emphasising the hollows in his cheeks, the dark smudges beneath his eyes. His life was in a chaos and she knew what that felt like. He'd once seen that in her, and he'd come to sit with her so that she was not alone. Now she longed to go to him, kneel by his chair and stroke his forehead, temples.

Now. Now was the moment...

'Kit—'

He started as she said his name. 'Sorry... Being your butler has been the better part of my day. I asked for a few minutes and I've overstayed that, but I need your help, Eve.'

What?

'I've seen how the people here respect you. How friendly you are with Peter Ngei.'

The moment had turned in an instant from unspoken intimacy to weird. Had she got it completely wrong?

'The respect is for my parents,' she said, hauling herself back from the brink of making a fool of herself. 'And Peter and I go back a very long way.'

'James told me that your parents lived here. Before the lodge was built.'

'You were talking about me?' she demanded.

'I really was concerned when you didn't return from your canoe trip,' he said, 'but when I raised my concerns with James, he explained that the village had arranged a surprise for you.'

'Yes...' It had been a day for surprises. 'I had the shock of my life when I realised that it was Peter at the business end of the canoe.'

'He came for you himself?'

'You sound surprised.'

'Clearly I saw a different side of him.' It was true, he did need her help to smooth over the mess he'd made of his initial meeting with Peter Ngei. The fact that it gave him the perfect excuse to spend time with her was a bonus. 'James told me that you lived here when you were a girl. That the lodge was built on the site of your parents' *boma*.'

'You two did have a nice chat.'

'It wasn't... James and I were talking about the history of the place.'

'Did he tell you that it was my mother who called it Nymba?' she asked.

'No. What does it mean?'

Eve, who had anticipated a difficult conversation about the future, instead found herself drowning in memories. Not all of them happy.

She stirred the melted honey into her tea. 'It's a Swahili word for home.'

'It must have been a shock when you saw your home at the auction.'

'This wasn't my home,' she said. 'This is a hotel built where our house once stood. There was a thick thorn fence around it to keep out predators. We had a lot of orphaned animals.'

'James told me about the baby elephants your parents reared, that the guests can walk with.'

'Daisy and Buttercup.'

'They're names for cows.'

'They were cow elephants. My dad's idea of a joke.'

'They say elephants never forget. Do you think they'll remember you?'

'Come with me and you'll see,' she said, her smile so unexpected that for a moment it took his breath away. 'That's if you have time. I imagine this is a business visit? Here today, gone tomorrow?'

'That was the intention,' he said. 'I'm here for the annual meeting with the Nymba Trust, who are our partners here. Unfortunately, Joshua Ngei is in hospital and, although his grandson runs the trust now, it seems that the meeting can't go ahead without him.'

'Joshua is the senior village elder. It's a question of respect.'

'Stuff you know and I'm having to catch up with, but that's okay. It gives me a chance to get to know the place.' Get to know her. He took a mouthful of coffee, then said, 'James said that your parents were studying the local elephant population.'

'Yes. I had hoped to follow in their footsteps, but life got in the way.'

'Life has a way of doing that,' he said.

'There are compensations.'

'Are there?' He sounded doubtful. 'What do you do, Eve?'

'I teach biology to high school students.'

'And your parents? Where are they now?'

'My father left to head up a new project in Sumatra. My mother stayed on here for a while. I came back that last summer and worked with her. I thought I'd be doing that until I joined her permanently, but then she left, too.' She looked at him. 'I had no intention of bidding at the auction, but when I saw Nymba on the screen it called to me.'

'Why did she leave? Your mother?'

Eve shook her head. 'My father had an affair with his research assistant. She went with him to Sumatra. This was his project and without him the money dried up. My mother moved to a new project in Central America. She was deep in the rainforest when she caught a fever and died before she reached the nearest hospital.'

'I'm sorry.'

'That goodbye has been said. This…'

He said nothing, waiting for her to find the words.

'When I left that last time, I thought I'd be

returning at Christmas. Instead I stayed with my father's parents in England. I broke my leg just before Easter so I had to stay with them again. My mother was supposed to go to Nantucket that summer, so I went there, but she was setting up the project in Central America and was too busy.'

'What about your father? Why didn't you visit him?'

'He had a new research project and a new woman in his life. The last thing he needed was a stroppy teenager underfoot.'

'That must have been tough.'

'There were other girls at school who were going through the same thing.'

'That doesn't make it better.'

No. And it was why she'd given up her dreams and chosen teaching. To be there after school and during the holidays for Hannah.

'I'm sorry, Eve.'

She waved a hand. Today had been very emotional and this wasn't helping.

Kit had looked her in the face and, after all, hadn't recognised her. It should have been a relief but, having got what she wanted, she was suddenly, stupidly furious. With her mother for dying, for losing the home she'd loved, the life she had dreamed of, and with Kit for being so blinkered.

Brown hair? Was that all it took?

'Why are you here, Kit?' she demanded. 'What do you want from me?'

'I'm sorry. I just wanted...' He lifted a hand in apology, clearly taken aback by her fierceness. 'My dad loves this place. My parents stayed here, on a second-honeymoon trip. All our other resorts are on the coast, the sea is our business, but they fell in love with Nymba. The lodge was doing well and I can see why. The setting is magnificent. What the trust badly needed was a partner with investment capital so that they could not only expand, but upgrade to meet the expectations of the luxury end of the market.'

'A match made in heaven.'

'So it would seem. Dad comes every year for a week to have a meeting with the Nymba Lodge Trust and relax. This year, as you know, he can't come, my brother is up to his eyes in the annual audit, so I stepped in.'

'So, have your meeting and relax.'

'I thought it would be a good idea to talk to

Peter Ngei before the meeting, to make sure there were no problems. James arranged for me to see him this evening and it all went downhill from there.'

Eve frowned. Peter had been full of his plans for the village, the school extension, Mzee's party, but hadn't mentioned anything about problems with Merchant.

'What happened?'

'I was distracted when he arrived and he was expecting to meet my father, not some playboy sailor.'

'Playboy sailor?' Eve, well aware that she had been the distraction, felt a stab of guilt. 'That's an outrageous thing to say.'

Except wasn't that how she'd always thought of Kit? Ignoring the dedication, the skill it must have taken to achieve so much in one of the world's toughest, most dangerous sports.

Judging him instead on the covers of gossip magazines.

'Did he really call you that?' she asked.

'A blue-eyed playboy sailor were his exact words.' He shrugged. 'It's water off a duck's back, Eve, but I've got to get this right. I've a lot of ground to make up with my family.'

'It's true, then, about the rift?' He glanced at her. 'It was all over the media just before you went on that round-the-world yacht race.'

'Dad was furious with me for entering. He said it was time I stopped messing about in boats and started using my name to support the business.'

'That was harsh. You must have already brought an enormous amount of publicity and prestige to the resort. I saw your gold medal beside your photograph in the entrance hall.'

'I gave it to him. I brought it back from London and gave it to him. He thought that was it, that I'd come home, go to college, join Merchant and wait for him to retire in twenty years…'

'Instead you did it again in Rio.'

'A two-hander that time, with Matt. After that there were other races, but when I announced I was taking part in the single-handed round-the-world yacht race he totally lost it.'

'Maybe he was scared for you,' Eve suggested, remembering how she'd felt watching the yachts put out to sea for the hardest race in the yachting calendar on the evening news.

Up to sixteen weeks alone, not touching land, storms, whales, icebergs...

How she'd felt when he was missing.

'Imagine how you would have felt in his place,' she said.

'I had a taste when I got the phone call from Brad saying that Dad was seriously ill, but when you're young you think you're indestructible.' There was a long silence and she knew he was thinking about Matt Grainger. A year or two older than him, with everything to live for. Eventually he stirred, looked at her. 'I told my dad that I wasn't prepared to spend the rest of my life showing my face at resorts and shaking hands with the guests like some trophy he'd won.'

'No one can hurt you like family,' she said.

'You've been there?'

'Not quite like that. Your dad wanted you to be with him, mine didn't even bother to come to my mother's funeral. I know they weren't married any more, but I asked him to come. I needed him there.'

She'd needed someone.

What she'd got was Kit.

And Hannah.

'When he didn't come, I told him I no longer considered him my father and blocked my bank from accepting any more direct transfers from him.'

'What did he do?'

'Nothing that made any difference to me.'

'And your grandparents?'

'They moved to Spain.'

'In case you made a habit of breaking limbs?'

She smiled as she was meant to. 'Something like that. I'm so sorry you lost your friend, Kit.'

'He was my sailing brother. I should have seen what was happening to him. Instead I was on the other side of the world talking to race sponsors…' He was looking out into the darkness. 'Lucy went to give him a shout when he didn't turn up for training one morning. She found him lying on the floor, stone cold, a needle in his arm.'

'Poor woman,' Eve said, thinking of the tenderness with which he'd held Lucy… 'You are both doing a lot to raise awareness, raise funds. And you turned up when your family needed you.'

'And I'm still making a mess of it.'

'You're here when you'd rather be at the far

end of the world at the helm of a multimillion-dollar racing yacht.' Winning another trophy.

Had her judgement been way off all round that summer? She hadn't been in the best place. Throwing herself into the arms of a total stranger had been totally out of character.

But then neither had he.

Forced to choose between his chosen career and his family business, he'd set off on that round-the-world race determined to prove something, even if it killed him. And it very nearly had.

There had been times when she'd wondered if it was just Kit's bad luck to be in her way when she'd lost it that night or whether any reasonably attractive man would have done.

She was about to turn his world on its head; the least she could do was try and help him.

'Peter is a decent man,' she said. 'Maybe you should suggest a fishing trip, sit quietly for a couple of hours, drink a couple of beers… You do know how to fish, don't you?'

'You put your toe in the water and wait for a bite?'

'Only if you're fishing for crocodiles.' She sighed. 'I'm not sure that I can help, Kit. The last time I saw Peter was the day my mother drove us both into the city. I was fourteen and going back to boarding school. He was just starting his second year at university. He was charming, glamorous and I had the world's biggest crush—'

There was a rattle of china as the teapot fell to the floor and smashed, and Kit let out an expletive.

'Sorry... I got a lapful of coffee.'

Eve leapt up to grab a towel from the pile stacked beside the bath, handing it to Kit as he abandoned the wet chair.

'Look out!'

His shout came too late as something that had been lurking beneath the towel leapt to her shoulder where, unless she turned to face it, all she could see was a dark shape.

She screamed as it brushed against her neck, her cheek, reduced in seconds from a grown woman who could handle anything to a gibbering wreck.

Kit knocked the creature away, sweeping it off the deck and out into the dark, and then gathered her in as she sagged, trembling, against him.

'Shh… It's okay…it's gone… I've got you…'

It had been seconds, it had felt like years, but his arms were around her, supporting her as she clung to him.

'Are you hurt?' he asked. 'Did it bite you?' She whimpered. 'Can I check?'

She nodded into his chest, not moving as he lifted her hair to examine her neck. 'I can't see any marks or swelling. Let's just…' He eased back her robe to expose her shoulder and went very still.

'What is it? Have you found something?'

'Yes,' he said, his thumb grazing her back a few inches below her shoulder, 'but it's nothing to worry about. Just a butterfly.'

'Oh.' Her stomach clenched as she realised what he'd found, and she forgot all about the hairy-legged spider. 'The stupid things you do when you've had one glass of Prosecco too many…'

'Oh?'

'It was a post-graduation party. A group of us decided we should mark the occasion with a tattoo.'

'And did you all go for a visual pun?' he asked, 'or was that just you? Only that looks to me like a red—' he turned from his examination of her shoulder to look straight into her eyes '—admiral.'

'Kit...'

'Don't! Don't say a word... Not until I've done this.'

She thought he'd been holding her close, but this was a whole new level of intimacy and she knew she should stop it but, even as her brain was scrambling for the word she needed, his mouth came down on hers like lava on ice and the only word hammering in her head was *yes, yes, yes...*

CHAPTER SEVEN

RAIN AFTER DROUGHT, feast after fasting, wind after a flat calm…

Kit was going to wait, give Eve time to decide when, if, she ever acknowledged what had happened between them, but the butterfly changed everything.

She might have disappeared after their night together, but she had not forgotten. She did not want to forget, or why would she have had a permanent reminder inked into her skin?

And her response to him was not one of reluctance. It was everything he'd ever dreamed of during long nights alone because, despite the many lovely women he'd met, who'd smiled, saying yes with their eyes, no one else would ever do.

He'd lost count of the times he'd turned at the glimpse of red hair on a slender whip of a girl, but it was never that pure red. Never the right girl. And in the years that had passed since that

unforgettable night in his cabin, she had ma-
tured into an infinitely desirable woman.

Was the woman as impetuous as the girl he'd
met on the beach?

The first time had been frantic, clothes coming off as they'd raced up the steps to the cabin,
already naked as he'd kicked the door shut,
tearing open protection with his teeth.

They hadn't made it to the bedroom, let alone
the bed. She'd been on him, desperate for raw
physical contact, the primeval heat of a man
inside her. It had been explosive, blow-your-
mind sex that had left them breathless, staring
at each other in stunned wonder.

And then he'd kissed her.

The second time had been dreamlike; a slow,
sensually devastating exploration. Tasting,
breathing in the scent of her skin, discover-
ing where touch was rewarded with a moan of
pleasure, how to bring that moan to scream-
ing pitch.

He'd never felt so powerful or so humbled…

Sexually sated, they had turned to food, cooking pasta naked at the stove, dripping sauce
on their bodies as they ate, licking it off each
other, abandoning food for a deeper hunger.

They'd talked about nothing, music, films, books; no family. They'd laughed, made love again and some days he thought they might still have been there but for that damned beach party, the crashing knock on the door that could only mean trouble.

There was no landline at the cabin and he didn't have the number of her cell phone to let her know what had happened.

His one hope was that she knew who he was, would give him a chance to explain. But there had been no call. Never so much as a glimpse of the bright curls that were now tangled around his fingers. Of the woman he was holding so close that he could feel her heartbeat.

It was a kiss he never wanted to end because he had no idea what would come next and it was Eve who broke the connection. She pulled back to look at him and for a moment he saw everything he'd ever dreamed of in her eyes. Then, with the slightest shake of her head, she eased away.

His hand slipped from the curls to momentarily cup her cheek.

Her wrap, where he'd checked for a spider bite, had slipped down, exposing rather more than her shoulder. He longed to slide his hand around her breast, knowing that a touch to her nipple would bring a gasp to those sweet lips, bring her closer so that she would feel what he was feeling.

Instead, not taking his eyes from hers, he lifted her wrap back into place and took a step away.

For a moment neither of them moved, then Eve, having tightened her belt around her, got down on her knees and began to pick up the pieces of the broken teapot.

Which answered any question he cared to ask about her impetuosity.

It had been a hot kiss, the kind with only one destination, but, while her body had been with him, her brain was still engaged and, from the careless way she was picking up the broken china, she was angry. But not, he suspected, with him.

'Leave it. You'll cut yourself.'

She carried on and he joined her, picking up the smaller pieces and putting them into a saucer.

'Where did you go...?' He looked up. 'I want to call you Red, but you aren't red any more. Why have you covered up that gorgeous colour?'

'Maybe this is my real colour.'

'I think I would have noticed,' he said, and regretted it the minute her cheeks flooded with colour.

She abandoned the broken china and sat down as if her legs were about to give way. 'If we're talking about vanishing tricks, where did you disappear to, Kit?'

Attack being the strongest form of defence? But it was a fair question and his would wait.

'There was some trouble on the beach,' he said, finishing the job of clearing up. 'My brother and a couple of other boys turned up late and got into a fight over a girl.' He placed the saucer on the table but remained on his feet. 'By the time I arrived there was an ambulance and a cop car at the scene and my brother was being read his rights.'

'Oh.' Her shoulders sagged a little. 'I'm sorry. That was my fault. If you'd been there—'

'If there's any blame to go around I think I'm second on that list. Right after Brad. He was lucky to get away with a black eye and community service.'

'Community service?'

'Brad and his friends had been drinking. They'd taken to their heels at the first sound of a siren. My idiot brother had been floored by a lucky punch. No one was prepared to give up names, including Brad.'

'Sit down, for goodness' sake, you're giving me a crick in the neck.' She waved impatiently at the seat beside her and, when he'd obeyed, said, 'It must have been hard, being the younger brother of someone who was world famous at sixteen.'

'He loved sailing, but he stopped when I was picked for the team.'

'Was he good?'

'We all learned to swim before we could walk and sail as soon as we could stand up in a boat.'

'But he was always playing catch up.'

'And I never slowed down to give him a chance.' He shook his head. 'I can't change the past, but he had the guts to change his future. He stopped being an ass, knuckled down to work. He knows the Merchant business inside out and it's obvious that he's been taking the strain for a while. He needed help and I should have been there.'

'How is your dad? Really?'

'His stroke was catastrophic. Not so much the loss of movement. That's distressing enough but gradually coming back. Speech is taking longer, although on the upside he can't tell me that he doesn't need me.'

'I'm so sorry.'

Eve reached out a hand to him in a sweet gesture of empathy. He desperately wanted to take it, hold it, but every instinct warned him her touch would be brief and quickly withdrawn.

'It's coming back, slowly,' he said, 'but he wasn't making a lot of sense and the lawyers produced his written instructions that I was to act as CEO in the event that he was ever incapacitated.'

'That's tough. On both of you.'

'Punishment may come late,' he agreed, 'but it comes.'

'That's how you see it? Not a statement of his trust in you?'

Kit stretched out his neck, easing out the tension, then shook his head.

'My sister reminded me when I spoke to her today that it's not all about me. He wrote the instruction right after Brad's court hearing; a threat to make him get his act together and it worked. I assumed he'd torn it up long ago. Brad is convinced that when Dad recovers sufficiently to make his wishes known, he'll choose me.'

'If he does, it's because he wants you home.'

He stared at her. She lifted her eyebrows, inviting him to think about it.

'I… It's not my life.'

'He won't be around for ever, Kit.' In the moonlight he saw her throat move as she swallowed, and her voice snagged a little as she said, 'You've had a great career, won every trophy going. What's left but to repeat yourself?'

His turn to swallow hard. 'I'm not…'

'What? Ready to play second fiddle to your brother?'

'Not cut out to sit behind a desk and run a resort business.'

'You're not sitting behind a desk now,' she pointed out. 'Have you given any thought about what you'll do when you retire from the sport?'

Retire? He wasn't thirty. He had years ahead of him. As soon as his dad was well enough to listen to reason…

'Why are we talking about this?' he demanded.

He wanted to talk about her. About them. About Nymba Lodge, for heaven's sake!

'This *matters*.'

She said it with a fervour that made him wonder just how much it had hurt her to be sent away from the home she loved to the bleakness of boarding school.

'Boat design,' he said. 'Matt Grainger and I were talking about the three of us going into partnership.' One day. When they were old. Except Matt would never be old... 'There's some land on the far side of the Merchant Resort site that is perfect for a studio, workshops, a yard.'

'Three of you?'

'Matt, Lucy and myself.'

Lucy...

'She was in your crew as well.'

'She's as good a sailor as her brother. Matt's death has shaken her badly but she's started giving children sailing lessons at the Nantucket resort.'

'She's staying?'

Of course Lucy was staying. She hadn't flown all the way from New Zealand for a five-minute talk about her brother. She was not just beautiful, she shared his passion for sailing; she was everything that Kit could possibly want.

'Maybe the two of you should go ahead with the design business,' she said, before he could answer. 'If you told your father what you are thinking of doing, showed him plans, began to set things in motion so that he could see a day when you'd be there—'

'Slow down! That's years away.'

'Of course. I just thought…'

'You're making perfect sense and, yes, it matters but this, here and now, matters more. I looked for you, Eve, but I didn't know who you were, what your circumstances were, so I was discreet. I didn't want to cause trouble.'

'I'm sorry I misjudged you. I should have left a note but I ran away. You couldn't find me because I'd caught the early ferry back to the mainland and the first available flight back to London.'

'Because of me?'

'No, Kit, because of me. I was in a bad place. My mother had just died, no one knew what to say to me. My poor young cousins had their arms twisted to take me to that party.'

'I could see that there was something, but I swear I never meant—'

'I needed someone to hold me,' she said, cutting off his words. 'I'd never done anything like that before.'

'Nobody in the history of the world has ever done anything like that before, Eve. It was unforgettable.'

Unforgettable? For a moment the word filled her head before she managed, 'Maybe we were both in need of a hug that night.'

'Is that all it was? If it meant so little why did you pretend not to know me this morning? Did I imagine that kiss?'

'What did you expect me to say? Hi, Kit, remember me? We had a one-night stand about four years ago?' She ignored his reference to that kiss. It would never have happened but for a spider. And a butterfly.

'Is it Peter?' he asked. 'You seemed very close when you came back from the village.'

'Did we?'

Eve did her best to ignore the little heart flutter at the suggestion that Kit might be just a little bit jealous. She'd seen him holding Lucy with a tenderness that came from the heart rather than driven by the loins.

He might have kissed her as if one of them were going to war, but that was down to an adrenaline rush. A response to something that had happened a long time ago.

The first time had been magical, and now she knew why he'd disappeared, she wasn't going to destroy that memory with a mistake that they would both regret in the morning. Not when she still had to tell him about Hannah. Not when Lucy was waiting for him to start a new life with her.

'What does he do?' Kit asked.

'He's a lawyer in the Attorney General's office.'

'Still glamorous, then.'

'Oh, yes. Handsome, clever and one day he will be rich,' she agreed. 'He has it all. He's also thoughtful, kind, loves his family, adores his children—'

'He has children?'

'—and his lovely wife, Maria,' she added, finally. 'Peter might be a city lawyer, but the village will always be the home of his heart, which is why I know he'll do what's best for the Nymba Trust. That's why you're here,' she reminded him. 'To talk about the trust.'

'I knew who you were, Eve,' he said, ignoring her attempt to turn the conversation away from the past. 'Not at first. You covered yourself up pretty well.'

'Says the man who's grown a beard.'

He rubbed his hand across his chin. 'Maybe we're both hiding.'

He was getting too close and she needed daylight, distance and to be wearing more than a bathrobe when she told him about Hannah. 'I'm going to the village on Saturday for Mzee's party,' she said, rising to her feet, making it clear that it was time for him to go. 'You can come with me if you think that will help.'

'Thank you.' He lifted a hand, as if for a goodbye touch.

She didn't move. She didn't dare risk even that.

'Goodnight, Kit.'

He closed his hand, nodded as if he understood and walked away.

Eve waited until she heard the click of the gate before she released a long, shaky breath.

Ever since she'd arrived in Nantucket she'd

felt as if she'd been holding her breath. Waiting for the other shoe to drop. Finally, it had.

When he'd turned up with the tea tray and it had seemed that his arrival had nothing to do with the past, she'd felt just a little bit peeved.

He hadn't recognised her? Really?

She'd put on a few pounds and had rather more to show in the boob department than before she'd given birth to Hannah, but had she changed that much?

The hair colour had been to stop her standing out in the street, and this morning she'd been able to hide behind her hat and dark glasses, but up close did it make that much difference?

No one she'd ever met in Nantucket—and they had all been at her grandmother's funeral—had been fooled.

And neither had he but if it hadn't been for a spider, and the momentary madness of a tattoo party, they might still be walking around the elephant in the room.

Whatever the truth of the matter, her mind was now clear.

Her grandmother's cottage needed a lot of work before it could be put on the holiday rental market, which meant staying in Nantucket for the summer. But Mary, like her mother, was urging her to stay on and she'd already had a call from the head of the local high school—no doubt prompted by Mary or Martha—inviting her to come and see him.

Her father was in Sumatra and her British grandparents had decamped to the warmth of Spain; she had no family in England.

Nantucket was where her mother had grown up, where they had spent a few precious holidays together. There was family she was growing increasingly fond of, cousins for Hannah and, despite having kept a profile so low that she was practically invisible, the island was beginning to feel very much like home.

Kit might or might not stay on the island, but it was her future and that meant telling him that he had a daughter.

Tonight there had been too much emotion, too much going on. Added to that was the fact that he would almost certainly be home before her, and she didn't know how he would react to the news that he had a daughter.

The Merchants were a powerful local family and it had to be wiser to wait until she was back in Nantucket and had the chance to consult a lawyer before she told him about Hannah. After that he could decide whether he wanted to be a part of her life.

Her decision made, she picked up her laptop but, as she had a video call with her baby, chatting away, telling her everything that she'd been doing in an accent that was rapidly taking on a local twang, she wondered what it would be like to do that with Kit beside her.

CHAPTER EIGHT

KIT SHOWERED, BUT HIS body clock was still off balance. He pulled on a bathrobe and leaned against the rail of his deck.

Somewhere below him on the riverbank, a creature grunted but his gaze was drawn to where Eve's sky suite was located. It had been carefully placed so that it was impossible for him to make out more than the faintest glow from the solar lights of the walkway but, amongst the other noises of the night, he thought he heard her laughing.

Was she calling home? Or talking to the faithful Peter Ngei?

He barely had time to wonder before his own phone, kept strictly on silent at the lodge, vibrated in his pocket.

'Brad...'

'I'm sorry I missed you this morning. How are things going?'

'Not particularly well. The man who actually runs the trust expected Dad and wasn't too pleased to get second best.'

'Wow, that must have stung.'

'Fortunately,' he continued, ignoring the jibe, 'our auction winner, Genevieve Bliss, used to live here. She knows everyone, speaks the language and she's taking me with her to a village party on Saturday. I'll do my best to make a good impression.'

'You know what, Kit? Right now, I don't care what you do, I just want Dad back, talking, even if he is giving me a hard time.'

'Maybe you should tell him that.'

'I did, but he wants to hear it from you.'

Kit expected Brad to end the call, but he didn't and, after a moment, he said, 'Laura told me that you took Lucy down to the boathouse this morning. How did that go?'

'Oh, yes. We were talking and she offered to run a class for beginners. Kids. She seems keen.'

'She needs to get back on the water, and the youngsters will be in good hands.' More silence. Clearly Brad had something he wanted to get off his chest, so he kept talking. 'When you have a moment, could you get that information on that piece of land I told you about before I left?'

'Why?' he asked, suspiciously.

'It's not urgent. I was just thinking about the future. Setting up a yacht design partnership.'

'Wasn't that something you were planning to do with Matt Grainger? Are you thinking of going ahead on your own?'

'With Matt and Lucy. I was thinking of asking Lucy if she'd be interested in just the two of us going ahead. She always had such great ideas and she doesn't have much to keep her in New Zealand.'

'You and Lucy?' he said.

'Is that a problem?

Brad's parting two words, one unprintable, one in the affirmative, suggested that it was. It had been a day of ups and downs, but Kit was grinning as he video-called his mother and asked her to put her tablet in front of his father so that he could talk to him.

It was still dark when Eve, late, swallowed a mouthful of coffee before going outside to where the balloon was being inflated.

'Did you oversleep, Eve?'

Kit. Of course he'd be there. He was everywhere.

There was no reason why he should have told her he was coming on this trip and she pushed away the thought that he had decided to come because of her. It was the last thing she wanted.

'It's still dark,' she hissed under her breath as one or two of the other passengers glanced their way. 'In no way can I be said to have overslept.'

'You're not a morning person, then?'

'While you are insufferably cheerful when you've got up before dawn.'

'Sailors catch sleep when they can. It means that I'm good for tea and toast in bed.'

'Only if you stick around,' she muttered.

'I thought we were over that.'

'Over and so done.'

'It doesn't sound like it.'

'I thought you were here on business,' she said, changing the subject.

'This is business. The delay in the meeting is giving me the opportunity to experience everything we have to offer our guests.' He nodded in the direction of the horizon. 'It's going to be spectacular.'

In the few moments that they had been standing there, the sky had taken on an imperceptibly paler edge and, while she was an owl rather than a lark, she gave a little sigh. 'It always is,' she said, turning away to listen to the pilot as he began briefing them on the flight, explaining what to expect while in the air, what they would see, how to stand for the landing.

That done, they climbed aboard, men first to help their partners into the basket, which meant that Kit was holding out his hands to steady her as she jumped down to join him.

The other women had managed it gracefully. Feet together, soft knees.

Still half asleep and, yes, definitely not feeling the love at such an early start, Eve caught her heel on the edge of the basket and she fell hard against Kit. He was rock steady, gathering her up, holding her so that her breasts were pressed against his chest, her face tilted up to his. Far too close.

Heat raced through her body, her lips felt hot and swollen and his eyes had the same darkness as the night she'd thrown caution to the winds, inviting his kiss and a whole lot more. The same darkness as when he had kissed her last night.

'Are you okay?' He was still holding her, his expression unreadable. The man should play poker.

'Y-yes. Sorry. You're right. I'm not great first thing in the morning. Or the evening, come to think of it. Heel in basket, foot in hem, boot in mouth… Thanks for catching me.' She managed a rather shaky laugh as she eased away from his body. 'You can let go now.'

'If you're sure?' His hands were holding the tops of her arms, still steadying her. 'You seem, a little shaky.'

'There was no one around to force-feed me a croissant.'

'I've got a Lifesaver…'

She took the candy he offered as flame roared upwards, heating the air in the balloon and, as it began to rise slowly from the ground, instead of letting go, he put his arm around her shoulders as they turned to look out across the top of the trees.

'It would ruin everyone's day if you fell out of the basket,' he said, before she could object.

'It would certainly ruin mine,' she agreed. 'It's good to see that you're taking an interest in Nymba, despite the lack of wind and tide.'

'Your enthusiasm is infectious,' Kit said, the basket rising above the trees just as the sun edged over the horizon, creating long shadows that stretched across the savannah, and turning the river into a winding shimmer of gold.

'Magic,' Eve murmured, allowing herself to relax against him, stealing a precious moment of closeness as they drifted silently above grazing zebra and antelope.

'Magic,' he agreed, but when she turned to smile up at him, hoping that he was feeling it, too, he wasn't looking at the world beneath them but at her.

Even as she registered the fact, he took the sunglasses hooked over his shirt pocket, flipped them open and put them on, leaving her with the impression that he was the one hiding.

Someone exclaimed at the sighting of three giraffe, moving majestically along the riverbank.

'I had a close encounter with one of those yesterday,' he said, not to her, but to the entire group. 'I opened the siding on my deck and it was right there. Have you any idea how long their eyelashes are?'

'Long enough to make an entire chorus line

weep,' Faye said with a sigh and everyone laughed.

After that they all seemed to come together, bond in the experience, exclaiming as they rose high enough to see the curvature of the earth, catch a glimpse of the sun shining on a distant lake, see the range of hills between them and the capital in the west before the heat haze rose to obscure them.

'They're blue,' someone said. 'In England the hills are blue when it rains. Is it going to rain?'

The question had been addressed to Kit who, as a sailor, seemed most likely to know these things, but Eve said, 'In Africa the hills are always blue.'

Having established that she was the resident expert, they quizzed her on the animals they saw and she told them the local names: *twiga* for giraffe, *punda milia* for zebra, and then, as the balloon neared a rocky outcrop, *simba* for lion...

The others used a variety of equipment from heavyweight camera gear to their phones to film the pride of lions lazing on the rocks, but Eve was content just to look and so, it seemed, was Kit.

The big cats were watching the herds of ante-lope grazing quietly below them, undisturbed by the balloon. The male gave a mighty yawn. The herd was safe enough for now.

At the pilot's urging they all reached out to grab a 'lucky' leaf as they swooped low along the river before landing gently an hour later.

The long wheel base four-by-four and trailer that had been following them arrived as they were all helping to gather in the deflated bal-loon. It had brought along a hamper with cham-pagne and a picnic breakfast of smoked salmon, eggs, meat, cheese and pastries for breakfast.

Kit had been drawn into conversation with the men about yachting, leaving her with the women.

'You know Kit Merchant?' Faye asked, clearly impressed.

'I won a bid for this trip at a charity auction held at the Merchant Seafarer Resort in Nan-tucket that he was hosting. I had no idea he'd be here.'

'It's just coincidence?' Faye said, rolling her eyes. 'If you were to ask me, I'd say he has the look of a man who thinks he's the winner.'

'No,' she said, quickly, but knew she was blushing. 'He's here on business.'

'That would be Health and Safety.' The other woman, Chrissie, smirked. 'Your health and safety.' And the pair of them laughed as they fanned their faces with their hands and mouthed, *Hot...*

Protesting further would only make things worse, Eve knew, but when they returned to the four-by-four the rest of the party scrambled into the two front seats leaving the rear vacant for the two of them. Kit stood back as she climbed, self-consciously, aboard.

'Have you got enough room up there?' he asked the others.

Having been assured that they did, he climbed up after her and, as they bounced back to the lodge on barely there tracks, said, 'Thank you, Eve.'

'What f-f-for...?' She yelped as the vehicle hit a particularly deep rut and she was thrown sideways. Kit caught her hand, then put his arm around her.

Faye glanced back, grinning as she mouthed, *Health and safety.*

Except that this didn't feel safe. Not at all.

'For this morning. For being here. This kind of thing is not much fun unless you're sharing it with someone.'

'I suppose so.'

She hadn't shared very much with anyone in the last three years. She met her uni mates from time to time, but her life was so different from theirs. While they were out clubbing, dating, living from one drama to the next, she was reading bedtime stories, watching natural history and cooking programmes and going to bed early to cope with an early-rising toddler.

Sharing even those things would make them special.

Eve was quiet for the rest of the ride back to the lodge, but that was fine. He was content to sit like this. To know that they had the rest of the morning ahead of them, then lunch.

He was fairly sure that an afternoon nap was the order of the day after that, a chance to catch up on the predawn wake-up call and prepare for the night-time game viewing, with the chance of spotting a leopard.

He refused to allow his mind to wander into the realms of siesta fantasy, but then another bump threw Eve against him. His hand brushed against her breast as he fielded her and he felt a quiver of awareness ripple through her that answered his own stirring arousal.

She pulled away, and as soon as the vehicle drew into the Nymba compound she jumped down without waiting for help.

'See you for coffee by the pool, Eve?' Chrissie called.

'Great,' she said. 'See you later.'

Kit was held by the necessity of helping down the other women, of being a good host, thanking everyone for their company, and all he could do was watch her go.

'Richard and I are going night-time fishing with the locals this evening,' one of the men said, claiming his attention. 'You're welcome to join us, Kit.'

'Don't be silly, Jeff. Kit has far more interesting things to do than go fishing.'

'Really?' He looked at his wife in surprise. 'What?'

'Clueless,' she muttered, shaking her head.

Jeff shrugged. 'Well, the offer is open.'

It was what Eve had suggested. He doubted that Peter Ngei would be in the party, but it would be a chance to prove to the village that, while he was not his old man, he was a fairly decent human being.

'I'd love to come along. Thanks, Jeff.'

'Men,' Kit heard Faye mutter to her friend as she walked away. 'They are all totally clueless.'

She was right, he thought. He was still wondering why Eve had acted as if they'd never met. He'd heard her reason, but she was a confident woman; if anything, he would have expected teasing. If it really hadn't meant anything. But she'd run away at the auction, too.

The attraction was still there, as hot and urgent as ever... He'd been thinking that kiss had been like the first time, but he was wrong. That had been all about discovery. This time, when he'd kissed her, it had felt like coming home after a long journey.

At least for him.

Eve had pulled away, but then she had no reason to think that he wanted anything other than a repeat performance. Wham, bam, see you in another four years.

At least this morning, once she'd got over her predawn snippiness, she'd relaxed in the calm of the balloon's gondola, leaning against him as if it was the most natural thing in the world while they'd wondered at the earth unfolding below them.

In the air, with other people around her, she'd felt safe.

Now they were back on the ground she wanted to put some distance between them.

He could wait.

He knew how to be patient, tacking against the wind, teasing his boat forward even in a flat calm. He'd waited four years to find his Red and the last thing he wanted was for her to cut and run again.

James was waiting to greet them back at the lodge with coffee, juice and water. 'How did you enjoy the balloon trip, Eve?'

With every cell in her body vibrating from the ride back with Kit, the ease with which she'd slipped into closeness, Eve had hoped to make a quick getaway and grab a little recovery time.

Caught, she said, 'It was wonderful. The sunrise was spectacular, and we had a thrilling view of a pride of lions on an outcrop of rocks.'

'That's always good to hear. Photographs of

the big cats on social media are good for business.'

As the rest of the party joined her she slipped away to her suite, tossed her hat aside and took a very cool shower. It didn't help and she sat for a while, her entire body shaking with need.

She'd leaned against Kit in the balloon and she'd wanted him to hold her, wanted to feel his skin against hers, to be touched. To assuage the ache to hold him within her body that had stayed with her in the months after she'd left Nantucket.

It had only eased in those early months of motherhood, when sleep had been reduced to snatched minutes and exhaustion had focussed all emotion on a small, demanding infant who'd looked at her with Kit's blue eyes.

She'd done everything she could to distance herself from the memory, only to be caught out by photographs on the covers of glossy magazines.

His kiss, long moments when the world had gone away and every barricade she'd erected had come tumbling down, leaving her weak with longing, had brought it all surging back.

Kit, with his hand close enough to a nipple

throbbing for the stroke of his rough thumb, must have known that all it would have taken was one touch and it would have been that night on the beach all over again.

Instead he had covered her.

Not a playboy, but a *'parfit gentil knyght'*. A man who, when he'd looked for her, had taken care not to do anything that might embarrass her.

He was reckless, careless of his own safety, but he was a much better man than she'd given him credit for.

It wasn't Kit she was hiding from up here in her suite, it was herself.

This trip had been a chance to relive that last holiday with her mother, reach back to precious memories, but this wasn't the Nymba of her childhood. It wasn't even the Nymba of that last summer with her mother.

She had chosen to remember it as a magic time, and it had been, but her mother hadn't asked her to come, hadn't wanted her to come. Busy with what had later transpired to be the final details of the project and with papers to write, her mother had encouraged her to go and visit her grandparents in Spain.

It was she who'd insisted on coming, saying that she wanted to help.

Had her mother given in out of guilt for having sent her away? She could have come home after the Nymba project, they could have lived together in the London flat, done the things her friends did with their mothers. But she'd already chosen the dangers of the Central American rainforest rather than her only child.

Eve had, she realised, made a conscious decision not to be like her mother, and yet here she was chasing the past when she could be at home with her daughter, tucking her into bed, reading her stories.

She would have video-called her, just for a glimpse of her sweet face, but they would all be asleep in Nantucket. Instead she took out her photo wallet and vowed to her baby that she would never again be the mother who put her own desires, wishes, above those of her child.

CHAPTER NINE

KIT PULLED TWO loungers into a shady spot at the end of the infinity pool. With her colouring, Eve wouldn't want to be in the sun.

He sent a couple of texts—one to his dad telling him what he'd done that morning, what he'd seen; one to Lucy asking her if she wanted to stay in Nantucket and, if so, would she be interested in going ahead with the design partnership they'd talked about.

Then he opened a book and waited.

It was about twenty minutes before Eve finally arrived, a long beach wrap over her swimsuit, her face shaded by her hat, her eyes hidden behind dark glasses.

She looked around but all the other loungers were in the sun and Chrissie, clearly a sunworshipper, called out, 'Kit sorted you out some shade.'

She waved an acknowledgement but took a breath that was as much mental as physical before joining him. 'I was concerned you'd get fried,' he said.

'That is very thoughtful.' She sat down, stretched out, produced an eReader from the bag she was carrying. 'I imagine it's a problem when you're at sea. What are you reading?'

He held up his book so that she could see the frozen ship on the cover and the title *Endurance*.

'Shackleton. The man who navigated across six hundred miles of the most dangerous sea in the world in an open boat. Just up your street.'

'You know about the expedition?'

'Our school houses were named after explorers. Stanhope, Kingsley, Shackleton and Livingstone. Two women and two men. They were hot on equality.'

'I'm glad to hear it,' he said, waving over a steward. 'What would you like to drink?'

'Iced coffee, please.'

'Two iced coffees, please, Jonah,' he said, then turned to her. 'So how was boarding school?'

'They did their best,' she said, 'but it was cold, it rained all the time, there was no freedom, no animals and no mother.'

'You hated it.'

'I hated not being here.'

'I don't suppose your parents had much choice.'

'I'm sure that's how they saw it. It's not one I'd ever make.' She stood up, slipped off her robe to reveal the stunning curves only hinted at beneath the shapeless bush gear she'd been wearing. 'I'm going to cool off.'

He watched her power up and down the pool for a few minutes before he joined her in the water, matching his speed to hers as he swam alongside her.

'Why are you so angry,' he asked as they reached the end of the pool.

She stopped. 'I thought sailors were superstitious about learning to swim.'

'A superstition they realised was bunkum the moment they fell overboard. Why are you so angry?' he repeated.

She propped her chin on her arms, looking at the heat haze dancing across the savannah. 'They say you should never go back.'

'You regret coming here?'

She sighed. 'I came here on a wave of nostalgia for some golden past and it's great catching up with people I grew up with.'

'But?'

'Memory blurs the edges. I remember the animals, the freedom, those special moments with my mother.' She turned away from the view. 'She was adorable. Everyone loved her and there are sweet moments, but she was always busy, always working. Sometimes she and my father were gone for days. It was Ketty who took me to school, made sure I was fed, who was always there for me.' She dashed a tear from her cheek. 'The last holiday here with her is a precious memory, but even then her mind was on the future. All she could talk about was her new project. I was studying zoology so that I could be with her, be part of her life...'

He opened his arms and she came into them, laying her cheek against his shoulder. 'I miss her so much, Kit.'

Warm tears spilled against his skin as he held her and for a moment they were the only two people on the planet.

'I'm sorry,' she said, pulling away much too soon, wiping her face with her hand. 'I don't know where that came from.'

'I imagine that coming here has opened up feelings that you've been keeping bottled up for a long time. It's not easy to admit feeling angry with someone who's dead.'

She lifted her head to look at him, tears clumping her lashes together. 'Are you angry with Matt?'

'When I saw him, afterwards, I just wanted to grab hold of him, shake him for being so stupid. Demand to know why he hadn't trusted me...' He shook his head. 'The truth is that I was angry with myself for not being there, not seeing what was happening.'

'You're making a difference, Kit. People will live because of what you've done.'

'I hope so.' He looked down at her. 'Are you done punishing the water?'

She nodded, and they returned to the shade of their loungers.

'So what *are* you reading?' he asked, as she dried herself off and began to apply more suncream.

'Under the Sea Wind.' She looked up. 'Rachel Carson.'

'My grandmother knew her. She stayed at the beach cabin when she was on the island.' He nodded at the bottle of sun lotion. 'Do you want me to do your back?'

She hesitated a moment. 'If you wouldn't mind.'

He sat beside her.

'Does your interest in a local author mean that you're considering staying on the island?' he asked to distract her as he slipped the straps of her costume over her shoulder and began to smooth the cream across her shoulders and down the deep scoop of her costume.

'Nana died recently. I'm sorting out her cottage.'

'She left it to you?' Her skin shivered under the roughness of his touch. 'Sorry about my hands. Your friend Peter might think I'm a playboy but the calluses tell a different story.'

He offered her back the cream but as she took it she held onto his hand, stroking her thumb over two crooked fingers. 'Not just the calluses. These were the fingers you broke on a round-the-world race. You had to lash them together with gaffer tape until they mended.'

'You were watching?'

'The whole world was watching. You could have died, Kit.' She looked up, her eyes searching. 'You must have known you wouldn't win so why did you carry on?'

The temptation was to shrug, as if it weren't important, but this was Eve, who'd just opened herself up to him in the most intimate way. She deserved more than his usual casual brushing aside of the pain, hardship, loneliness of those months.

'It's the ultimate goal,' he said. 'Something I'd dreamed of since I was a kid. Sponsors want winners, or a story, and I knew that if I gave up, I might never have another chance.'

And that, he thought, was why Matt had hidden the pain he was suffering. Because if he was seen as damaged, a liability, he might never get another chance to crew the ultimate yacht.

'You gave them headlines they could only have dreamed of,' Eve said, breaking into the uncomfortable realisation that there wasn't a whisker between them... 'Would you do it again?'

His hesitation was answer enough and Eve let go of his hand, put on her sunglasses, picked up her reader and lay back in shade.

Would he?

Memory blurred the edges.

In his head he knew there was pain, exhaustion, the same boring food over and over, but there was the exhilaration of taking the worst the elements could throw at you and winning through.

He wouldn't do it now but maybe, ten years from now, in a yacht he'd designed himself...

'Are you hungry?'

Eve had been staring at the same page for what seemed like for ever. She had been warming to the idea that she had misjudged Kit. He was a kinder and more thoughtful man than she had given him credit for but, while he was home for now, he'd made it plain that he had no interest in the family business.

His business was with the sea. Sooner or later the siren call of the ultimate challenge would be irresistible, and the next time Hannah would be old enough to understand.

Would she be watching and waiting for her daddy to come home with terror? Or would she be hooked?

It was a relief to look up and see that the pool had been deserted and guests were beginning to gather at the bar for pre-lunch drinks.

'I didn't realise it was so late.' She closed

her reader and dropped it in her bag. 'I need to change.'

'You will come back?' he asked.

'Will you come and find me if I don't?' She'd meant it as a challenge, but it had come out sounding more like an invitation. She wasn't hungry, not a bit, but she said, 'Just give me ten minutes.'

She was halfway to the steps when she heard a splash.

'What have you done to that poor man?' Faye, perched on a barstool, asked as she passed.

'It's complicated,' she said, without thinking, as they watched Kit, his powerful, sun-bronzed shoulders gleaming as he drove through the water.

'On the contrary, that's the simplest feeling in the world, sweetie,' Faye said, with a little sigh.

She knew that. Had once surrendered to that most basic instinct without a thought. It was thinking that messed with your head.

It was too early to call home and talk to Hannah, but Eve took a photograph of a monkey in a nearby tree and sent it to her with a load of kisses. By the time she returned to the terrace twenty minutes later, Kit was sitting on a stool, hair damp, but wearing a short-sleeved shirt and a pair of chinos.

'What would you like to drink?' he asked.

'Just water,' she said.

'Still? Or will you risk a little fizz?' His face was poker-straight but she knew when she was being teased.

It had been so long since anyone had dared to tease her. Had held her. Had made her feel that she was not just Hannah's mother, but a woman, and she smiled despite her determination to keep her distance.

'I'll risk the fizz,' she said, but grabbed a vacant seat between Chrissie and a new arrival when they sat down to lunch. Kit raised an eyebrow but took a seat amongst the rest of the new arrivals and barely looked in her direction once.

He left before she did, touching her shoulder lightly as he passed, his fingers brushing over the butterfly hidden beneath her shirt, but saying nothing.

She watched him walk away but he didn't look back. She didn't see him again until, two hours later, he was waiting by the vehi-

cle that would take them to the part of the re-
serve where they would walk with Buttercup
and Daisy.

'It's just us?' she said.

'More than two and the elephants can get
spooked. You have to book well in advance to
have this privilege. Fortunately, it was part of
the package you bid for,' he said, offering his
hand to help her up in the seat.

'So how did you get lucky?'

'Everyone else came in pairs.'

The ranger who cared for the elephants had
been at school with her and she hugged him,
asked after his family, introduced him to Kit.

By then, Daisy, always the most curious, lowered her head and touched her gently with the
tip of her trunk.

Eve put up her hand to rub it, murmuring
softly as she rested her forehead on the great
beast. Buttercup, not to be outdone, curled her
trunk around her.

'Is she hugging you?' Kit asked.

'Elephants never forget,' Eve said, taking his
hand, encouraging him to touch first Daisy and
then Buttercup, telling them his name, reassur-
ing them that he wouldn't hurt them.

They touched him, responding with happy little snorts.

'I think they can smell me on you,' she said.

'It's vanilla,' he said, looking at her, rather than the elephant. 'The memory of it stayed with me for weeks.'

For a moment Eve couldn't breathe, then she managed a slightly shaky, 'It's more likely that you got a blast every time you passed a bakery.'

'No, it was more complex than a cupcake.' He glanced at her. 'It was there after I caught you falling at the auction.'

'It's my perfume, Shalimar,' Eve confessed. 'My mother always wore it and she'd sometimes put a drop on my wrist. I bought a tiny bottle in the airport duty free on my way to school. I wasn't allowed to wear it, but I put it on my pillow. With you it's the sea that's become part of you. With me it's Shalimar.'

'And like the elephants, I have never forgotten it,' he said, taking her hand as they began to move off.

Eve skipped the early morning game drive and had a lie in, sitting up in bed on the deck, putting together pictures Kit had taken of her with the elephants, planning to send them to Hannah. Afterwards, he'd handed her phone to the ranger and asked him to take a photograph of the two of them.

They were standing with Daisy. She was making a fuss of Daisy and laughing, but Kit was looking at her in a way that brought a lump to her throat. In a way that she wouldn't want anyone else to see. She knew she should delete it, but then the phone rang, making her jump. An unknown number. Normally she would have let it go to voicemail, but it could be a call from home. Hannah…

'Eve Bliss.'

'I hope I didn't wake you.'

'I…' It was okay, no drama, just Kit. 'How did you get this number?'

'I sent a photograph of you with the elephants to my phone. We're going to put up a board with pictures showing everyone who won a bid at the auction having a good time. That one is going to be a winner.'

'What do you want, Kit?'

'I kept an almond croissant for you, but you didn't turn up for coffee this morning. I'm just being a good host and checking that you're okay.'

'I'm preserving my energy for the party. How was your evening? Did you catch any fish?'

'You doubt it?'

'Half a dozen men in a boat with a case of beer and basket of food. Oh, yes, I seriously doubt it. Was Peter there?'

'No. He went into the city to collect his grandfather, but he sent a message to say that we're having the trust meeting this afternoon, before the party.'

'Well, that's good news. You'll be able to go home tomorrow.'

'I could stretch to another day or two. I haven't had a canoe trip yet and I'm told there are waterfalls that shouldn't be missed. Would you like breakfast in your suite this morning?'

She sighed. 'You're outside my suite, aren't you?'

There was a tap on her gate. 'Service, Miss Eve.'

'Oh, for heaven's sake.'

She closed her phone as Kit carried a tray across the deck and laid it on the table.

'Coffee, orange juice, and since I wasn't

sure what you'd like I brought eggs Benedict, pancakes, and avocado on toast with poached eggs.'

'That's a shocking waste!'

'I was hoping you'd say that. Will you come over here?' he asked. 'Or shall I join you over there?'

'Go!' she demanded. 'Now!'

'Can I take the eggs Benedict?'

If she'd had anything to hand, she'd have thrown it at him.

CHAPTER TEN

KIT, CHECKING IN to update Brad, got a call divert to his sister. Again.

'Hi, Laura. How's Dad?'

'He's still struggling to find the right words. The stuff he's coming out with is actually pretty funny. He and Mom are doing a lot of laughing.'

'Yes, I got that when I called on Skype yesterday.' Realising that she was struggling with tears, he said, 'You know recovery from stroke is really good these days.'

'It's going to take months, Kit. He may never get it all back.'

'Dad's a fighter.'

'I know. What are you up to?' she asked with determined brightness, and he didn't have to be there to see that she was making an effort to put on a smile. She was a fighter, too. 'Apart from ruining Brad's unusually good mood. Sitting around in the sun watching the wildlife?'

'Pretty much,' he said, looking down at a family of elephants playing in the river. 'Hot-air ballooning, fishing, walking with elephants and today it's the village elder's birthday and I've been invited to the party.'

'Working really hard, then.'

'You can come with Dad next year. What have I done to upset Brad? Where is he anyway? I thought he never left his desk but I've yet to find him there.'

Laura cleared her throat, meaningfully. 'Lucy wanted something in town.'

It took him a moment to process that. 'Are you telling me that he left his office to take her to the store?'

'When they came back from the boathouse she said, "Brad, I really need some of my special hand cream…"' Laura put on a breathy *I'm so helpless* voice that was so unlike Lucy that he laughed. 'You think I'm kidding? I'm telling you he was walking her to his car before I could ask him to bring me some chocolate.'

Actually, that wasn't funny. He didn't believe for a moment that the scene had gone down like that. Lucy might have said she was going to walk into town to get some hand cream, but that Brad had volunteered to take her bothered him.

'Do you want to hear the gossip about your Miss Bliss?' Laura asked, breaking into his thoughts.

'She's not my anything,' he said, shutting his mind firmly against the word *gossip*. He knew what that was worth.

He'd held this image of her in his head, his heart for so long and there had been a moment when he'd held her, kissed her, when it had seemed as if the wait was over.

Nothing could be further from the truth.

The falling-into-bed attraction was there, as strong as it had been that first night, but it was more than that. Just being with her was time well spent.

He'd missed her first thing. Her smile, the easy banter. She'd sent him away with a flea in his ear for his cheek when he'd taken up breakfast, but it had been worth it for the vision of her, mysterious behind the gauzy mosquito net, lying back against a pile of pillows. Her shoulders bare but for tiny straps that held up whatever she was wearing beneath the sheet, her hair a tumbled mass of curls.

Not his anything. But, if he was lucky, she might be his everything.

'I have to go,' he said. 'Give my love to Mom and Dad.'

Kit loaded his contribution to the party in the back of one of the lodge's vehicles and returned to Reception. Eve was standing in the reception area. She was chatting to James and she had her back half turned to him so she didn't see him stop dead in his tracks.

Her hair, a mass of loose curls, was glowing in a shaft of sunlight. It wasn't the clear bright red he remembered, but the colour she used was fading out, leaving it the soft shade of maple leaves in the fall. Make-up subtly enhanced her eyes, drew attention to her mouth and she'd abandoned the shapeless khaki bush gear for the party. The simple, elegant moss-coloured linen dress that reached her ankles would, he knew, exactly match the green in her eyes.

'Ready to go?' James asked, as he spotted him. She turned and for a split second, before she closed it down, he saw his own heart leap reflected back at him and it took him a moment to find his voice.

'Are these all yours?' he asked, indicating the large number of bags at her feet.

She lifted her shoulders fractionally in an apologetic shrug. 'I knew I'd be visiting the village, so I shopped for gifts before I travelled.'

'Is Peter here?' she asked, as he gathered them up in two hands. 'I didn't hear him arrive.'

'James has kindly loaned me one of the lodge vehicles so I sent him a message to say that we'd make our own way to the village.'

Eve raised an eyebrow. 'Grabbing back a little bit of control, Kit?'

Control? That was a joke. He was so out of control that, but for the touch-me-not force field around her, he'd be kissing the words right off her mouth.

His sexy Red had given him a night he'd never forgotten. Eve, he realised, had become so much more. Beneath the sexuality that she'd done her best to mask was an intelligent woman who'd seen through his motive as easily as through a pane of glass.

Eve, on the other hand, shimmered like a mirage…

'It's not about control,' he said, pushing the disturbing thought away as he stacked her bags on the back seat. 'It occurred to me that he wouldn't be able to relax and enjoy the party if he has to drive us back.'

'Actually,' she said, as she climbed up into the passenger seat, 'that's extremely thoughtful.' And his reward, as he started the engine, was to see the corner of her mouth lift in a smile. The real kind. She was fighting it, but she was losing.

Eve kept her eyes on the dirt road and Kit seemed unusually quiet. She'd sent him away this morning when having him stay, sharing breakfast with him, would have been a precious moment to remember.

Kit was going back to Lucy and, for Hannah's sake, they would need to be friends, or at least civil. The kiss could be excused as a response to the moment, but anything else could only lead to awkwardness, guilt.

He'd be gone tomorrow, giving her a few days to get her head straight, think about how she would tell him about Hannah. How she was going to tell Hannah.

The moment they arrived at the village the door was flung open and there was Ketty, older now, but arms open wide to embrace her as she jumped down.

The hug was a long shared moment, the silence filled with memories. Then, they were surrounded by excited children who she entrusted with most of the bags she'd brought. Two she kept.

'This is for you, Ketty. I'll go and give Mzee his birthday present, then I'll come and share out the rest.'

But Ketty was staring at Kit, who had opened up the rear of the vehicle and taken out a couple of cartons of beer.

'Ketty, this is Kit Merchant.'

'The young woman who took care of you when your mother was working?' Kit put down the beer. 'I've heard a lot about you, Ketty, from Eve and from James.'

'And I've heard much about you, Mr Merchant,' Ketty said before, with the briefest nod, she ushered the children away. 'I'll go and make tea.'

Eve, too shocked to hide her astonishment at such a cold reception, turned on him and said, 'What on earth have you done?'

He shook his head. 'I have no idea. Let's go and pay our respects to Joshua Ngei,' he said, reaching back into the vehicle for the box containing the bottle of whiskey he'd brought with him. 'If I survive that encounter maybe the frost will melt a little.'

The old man was sitting with his friends in the shade of a tree.

'Happy birthday, Mzee,' Eve said, placing her gift in his hands and kissing his cheeks, before wishing him a long life and good health. He opened the package and exclaimed with pleasure at the soft collarless cotton shirt she'd brought him. Then she turned to Kit, who had been standing back a little.

'Mzee, may I introduce my dear friend, Kit Merchant.'

He gave her a quizzical look before turning to Kit. 'I know your father,' he said. 'I am sorry to hear that he is not well.'

'He sends his warmest greetings with this,' he said, placing his gift of whiskey on the table beside the old man, 'and wishes he could be here to drink it with you.' Then he offered his hand, holding his arm respectfully, bowing as he repeated a traditional greeting.

Mzee looked at her, as if to check her reaction. Puzzled, she nodded, smiled, put a hand on Kit's back as if to enclose him within the group.

'Send your father my prayers for his return to health, Mr Merchant,' he said, accepting Kit's hand, before he indicated with a gesture that he should sit beside him. 'We hope to see him here again very soon.'

Kit caught her hand as she let it drop and gave it a brief squeeze, acknowledging the 'dear friend', then took the seat vacated for him next to Joshua Ngei.

'I hear you are a great fisherman, Mr Merchant.'

'My father is Mr Merchant, sir, I am just Kit,' he said.

'Then open the bottle, Kit, and we will drink a toast to Christopher Merchant.'

Eve lifted her hand to her mouth.

She had lived with an image of him in her head for so long. The passionate and tender lover. The man who could make her laugh when laughing was something alien. The man who could make her feel when she was numb. The man who had seemingly abandoned her, but had looked for her.

The blue-eyed playboy sailor who regularly appeared on magazine covers, always with a glamorous woman at his side.

A man whose life was the sea.

The father of her child.

This skill as a statesman was yet another layer to this compelling man.

'Eve!'

She turned to see Ketty clutching the handbag she'd given her to her chest. 'It's so beautiful! Thank you.'

'I'm glad you like it,' she said, a little shakily, as they turned to walk across to where the rest of her gifts were waiting to be shared out, and she realised that all the women were looking at Kit.

'He is very pretty,' Maria said.

'He has a great ass,' one of the older women said. 'I'd be tempted.' They all laughed, everyone but Ketty, who just reached for her hand and squeezed it.

No one would let her help with the cooking,

so she and Maria kept the younger children amused until the trust meeting was over. Kit gave her an almost imperceptible nod and she let out a breath she hadn't been aware she was holding.

'Did Peter tell you we're building a science lab for the school?' Maria asked.

'He said, but the workmen were there so it wasn't safe to go in. I'd like to take a photograph of the plaque you've erected to my mother.'

They were joined by several women who were home from the city for weekend celebrations who wanted to see how the extension was progressing and, having admired that, they all took a nostalgic tour of the classrooms.

'Oh, look,' one of the women said, looking at the pinboard with photographs of all the pupils in the class. 'They have a photograph of you when you were here, Eve.'

Maria took a closer look.

'That's not Eve. She has green eyes. This is her little girl. Peter said you'd given a picture of her to the children yesterday,' she said. 'She is very like you as a child.'

'It's just the hair.'

The scent of the sea had warned her of his presence a split second before Kit spoke. Before he reached over her head and took the picture down to look at it more closely.

'This child is the image of my sister at the same age.'

She turned, her mouth working, but no words coming out. She didn't have to say anything. One look and he'd known.

'What is her name?' he asked.

Her tongue was stuck to the roof of her mouth and it took a moment before she could say, 'Hannah Rose Merchant Bliss.'

He glanced at her, a nod acknowledging the inclusion of Merchant. 'She's beautiful.'

'Yes.'

'When were you going to tell me?' he asked, those blue eyes unreadable, his voice even, unemotional. 'Were you ever going to tell me?'

The others, at a signal from Maria, had melted away, leaving them alone.

'No,' she admitted. 'I only came back to Nantucket because my grandmother was sick.'

The sun, which had lit up the room just moments before, had sunk behind the trees and his face was all shadows. 'That's why you dyed your hair. You were hoping I wouldn't notice you.'

'Your team blog said you were in the Southern Ocean, but I couldn't take the risk.'

'You actually checked?' Even, unemotional, frighteningly calm.

'Yes, I checked. I should have been long gone by the time you returned, but Nana died and I had to stay and deal with the cottage.'

'Of course, you told me that she left you her cottage.'

'No.' She shook her head. 'She knew I'd sell it. She left it to Hannah.'

'Why, Eve? Why would you do this? Why didn't you tell me?'

'Why do you think?' she demanded. 'You meet a girl on a beach, have a one-night stand, then disappear.'

'I told you my name. All you had to do was pick up a phone.'

'And what? Ask for the money to take care of it?'

He took a step back as if she'd slapped him.

'You weren't hitting on me, remember? I jumped you and I chose to take responsibility for my own actions.'

'There were two of us in the room.'

'And then you left.'

He lifted a hand in a gesture at once helpless and exasperated. 'You know why!'

'Now I know. Then...' She shook her head, willing him to understand.

'Then you thought I'd had a good time and walked out on you.' She didn't want to tell him everything she'd thought. That was enough. 'Despite that, you chose to keep her,' he said, his voice softer.

'There was never any question about that, Kit. Hannah is my joy.'

'What about my joy?' he demanded. 'I have a child, a daughter, and you chose to keep her from me.'

Eve felt as if she was hanging onto reality by her fingernails. She'd been going to tell him, assure him that he didn't have to be involved, that he could walk away. That would have been better, but only marginally. She hadn't expected him to be angry. To feel cheated...

'I was going to tell you.'

'Why? Because I saw through your pathetic disguise?'

'Because I'm going to stay in Nantucket.'

'Too damn right you are,' he said, the cold calm finally breaking down.

'Kit... I was going to tell you, but not here. You're leaving before me—'

'And you thought I might take her?'

'I didn't know what you might do.'

CHAPTER ELEVEN

KIT BREATHED OUT an expletive and he sat on one of the class benches as if his legs could no longer hold him.

'She's my daughter, Eve, and I've missed so much of her life already. I didn't even get a say in her name.'

'I named her Hannah after my grandmother, Rose after my mother.'

'She had just died, hadn't she? Your mother. That's why you were in Nantucket. Why you looked so lost...' He shook his head. 'How on earth did you cope?'

'My mother got the London flat in a divorce settlement from my father. I lived there while I was at uni, and she left it to me, along with some money.'

'I didn't mean... How did you cope emotionally? With the pregnancy? The birth?'

'I was in the middle of my finals and I didn't realise I was pregnant until they were over.' She sat down on the bench opposite him. 'Truthfully, Kit? I was grieving for my mother, furious with my father and with my hormones shot to hell I might not have been entirely rational at the time, but the promise of a baby felt like a gift and for that I'll always be grateful to you.'

'Did you have anyone with you? At the birth?'

'The tattoo group rallied round. The one with the dragonfly is Hannah's godmother. They are scattered all over the world now, but they all considered themselves her honorary aunts and uncles.'

He took one last long look at the photograph and then slipped it in his pocket as he stood up.

'No,' she said. 'I gave that to the children. I have others you can have.'

'It finally explains the cold shoulder,' he said, as he pinned it back. 'Peter saw this photograph and when he brought you back to the lodge yesterday and saw us together, he guessed I was her father.'

'Because you both have blue eyes? That's a bit of a long shot.'

'He saw my shock when I recognised you and drew his own conclusions.'

'That jibe about the blue-eyed playboy.' She

swallowed down a lump the size of a golf ball in her throat. 'I thought at the time it sounded personal. I'm sorry, Kit. I'll explain.'

'No need. It was plain enough for everyone to see what you'd done.'

'I didn't want a scandal, Kit. My mother's death was all over the local newspapers. Can you imagine the gossip? My mother was hardly cold in her grave and I was having sex with a stranger on the beach. I was so ashamed—'

'Ashamed?' For a moment he looked furious then dragged his hand over his face. 'I'm sorry. I can't begin to imagine what you were feeling.'

'I was sure you were on tenterhooks waiting for the story to appear in one of the gossip magazines.'

'It would have made a change for one of them to be true.'

'Are you saying they were all made up?'

'I was young and stupid but they were mostly spun out of a grain of truth. No one knows that I'm Hannah's father?' he asked. 'Adding "Merchant" to her name was a bit of a giveaway.'

'I was in London, Kit, and the registrar was too busy to care what I called her. As far as the rest of the world is concerned, she is Hannah Bliss.'

'Not your family? Weren't your friends curious?'

'A secret shared is no longer a secret.'

'You told them you didn't know...'

She shrugged. 'A *Mamma Mia* moment.'

'That's the gossip my sister picked up. That you have a child whose father is something of a mystery.'

'You had your sister check up on me?'

'And chose not to hear what she'd discovered. More fool me. Not to worry, there's nothing like a wedding to gloss over the secrets of the bride.'

'What bride?' He didn't bother to answer. 'No,' she said. 'No way. I'm not... I won't...'

'I... I... I... This isn't about you any more, Eve. It's about putting Hannah first.'

'I do. I have,' she protested.

'And when she asked why she hadn't got a daddy? Or hadn't you thought that far ahead?'

She'd thought about it. She'd seen her baby's wrinkled forehead as she'd watched her cousins play with their father, the thought forming in her precious head.

'You can have all the access you want,' she said.

'You can bet your life I'll have access,' Kit said. 'Until the day you disappear back to London, taking her with you.'

'No!' she protested. 'I wouldn't do that.'

'You already did.'

'I told you, Kit, I'm going to stay on the island. I've got an interview for a job at the high school.'

'And who will look after Hannah while you're working? Who looked after her in London?'

'She went to an excellent day nursery. She loved it and I'm sure they have such things in Nantucket, so if you think you're going to marry me and I'll be a stay-at-home mom, think again.'

'Where are you living?'

'In Nana's cottage. Hannah's cottage.'

'I was looking for an address.'

'Oh. I see.' He waited and she said, 'Wisteria Cottage. It's in Paston Lane, just across—'

'I know where it is. It's been neglected.'

'It needs a coat of paint,' she admitted.

'It needs a complete renovation job. You can't stay there.'

'I have to. The cat won't move.'

'The cat?'

'Mungo. They tried to move him when Nana was in hospital, but he wouldn't eat.' He was clearly lost for words so she said, 'I'm working on it. I'm going to rent storage space so that I can clear out all the clutter and then—'

'Why don't you just get rid of it?'

'The cat?'

'The clutter.'

'The trustees have made it clear that it all belongs to Hannah. Nana and Grandpa's clothes. Cat-scratched furniture. Fifty years of paperwork…'

'That sounds like a fire hazard. We should get a ruling from the chief.'

We…

She pushed the temptation away. It was time to get real.

'You can't marry me, Kit. You're in love with Lucy.'

'What on earth are you talking about?'

'I saw you with her at the auction. I can recognise love when I see it. You're going into partnership with her, for heaven's sake.'

'You weren't thinking about Lucy when we kissed.'

'I wasn't thinking at all.'

The corner of his mouth lifted in a smile. 'That is the effect one hopes to achieve. If it makes you feel better, my brain wasn't entirely engaged, either.'

'Kit...'

'Is that the only reason you're saying no?'

'It's a pretty big one, don't you think?'

'There's more than one kind of love, Eve. I've known Lucy since she was a sailing-mad kid. I love her, of course I do, but like a sister.'

Eve now had a lump the size of a mango in her throat and couldn't speak.

'Is there anything else?' Kit asked. 'Speak now or for ever hold your peace.'

She shook her head. 'Maybe we should fly to Vegas and do it on the way home,' she said, not entirely flippantly.

'You'd deny me that, too? And what about Hannah? Do you imagine our daughter will forgive us if she isn't a flower girl at our wedding?'

We... Our... They were such magic words...

'Our daughter is a little young to know that she's missing anything, but her cousins would be absolutely livid.'

He nodded as if it were settled. It wasn't. He'd had a shock, his emotions were in turmoil but once they were home, he'd begin to think straight.

'It's gone very quiet out there,' he said, standing up and offering her his hand. 'Perhaps we should put in an appearance before someone passes out from holding their breath.' She nodded. 'It would help if you could manage a smile. If they think I've made you unhappy they might feed me to the crocodiles.'

She laughed, as she was meant to and, with her hand firmly in his, he headed for the door. Outside there was a wide semicircle of people waiting.

'As you will all have realised, Eve has today surprised me with the greatest gift imaginable, that of a daughter. In return I have asked her to marry me and she has made me the happiest of men by saying yes.' He turned to her, and, eyes hooded to hide his thoughts, and while she was still struggling with what had just happened, he kissed her.

It was brief, but emphatic and if, as a result, she clung to him just for a moment, while her knees remembered what they were for, it all added to the illusion that this was a happy-ever-after ending.

The announcement, the kiss, were greeted with a round of applause and then they were all heading back to the centre of the village where fairy lights had been strung in the trees, music was playing and, since it seemed to be expected, Kit took her in his arms and whirled her around the square.

It looked like one of those perfect moments. Lovers reunited, a wedding to plan, a new life waiting for them.

'Tears, Evie?' She did her best to blink them back as Ketty took her hand in both of hers. 'We are all thinking about your mother. She would be overjoyed to see you so happy.'

'Yes,' she said, and she reached into the very depths of her soul to dredge up a smile that would convince the world that it was the happiest day of her life.

* * *

It was late and the headlights piercing the darkness as they drove back to the lodge caught the reflections of eyes watching from the bush on either side of the track.

The party had been noisy and they'd left it in full swing, making the silence of the drive back to the lodge all the more intense.

'I have invited Peter and Maria to the wedding,' Kit said, at last. 'They'll stay at the Nantucket resort as my guests.'

'They needed convincing that you're doing the right thing?'

'A photograph would have done that.' He glanced at her. 'I thought you'd like to have them there.'

'I don't want anyone there.'

'You're still rooting for the Las Vegas option?'

'I'm rooting for the no wedding option.'

He stopped the four-by-four. 'You took a unilateral decision to deprive me of my child, Eve. The anticipation of waiting for her arrival, the anxiety of the scans, the joy of making a nursery, sharing the news, of being there when she was born.'

'I promise you, I wasn't feeling the joy,' she said, and immediately regretted it. The hours of discomfort, pain, had been forgotten in that first moment when she'd held her baby, seen the slightly puzzled look in those blue eyes, the surge of unconditional love. 'I... I thought I was doing the right thing for everyone.'

'I know, but it's a moment, a memory, I will never have. One of hundreds. Her first smile...'

'Her first projectile vomit,' she said.

'Her first step.'

'The panic of a temperature so high I called an ambulance, convinced she had meningitis.'

'Eve—'

'It was already going down by the time they arrived ten minutes later. She's had all her shots and is growing like a weed,' she said, reaching out to reassure him.

'I've never told her a bedtime story.'

'She didn't sleep for a year.'

'Her first Christmas.'

'She screamed the first time she saw Santa.'

'The first time she looked at me and said "Dada".'

Eve sighed. 'That's it. You win...'

'No, don't you see? I've lost and lost and lost.

I don't even know her birthday. Early August so... May?'

'The fifth.'

'Tell me about her, Eve. What does she like?' he asked.

'Like?'

'What colour, what food, what toys...?'

As Kit listed the things he didn't know about Hannah, Eve put her head in her lap, covering it with her arms to block out his voice, over-whelmed by guilt as she accepted the reality of what she'd done.

She'd said sorry, but saying it a hundred, a thousand times could never undo this.

'Eve...?'

She shook her head, but he lifted her arms, pulling her up. 'Look at me,' he insisted and then, wiping tears from her cheek with his thumb, 'Talk to me.'

'My father wasn't there.' The words came from nowhere.

'Your father? But I thought, you said... He and your mother worked together?'

'Yes, but did you hear anyone mention him today? He never went to the village. He didn't take a bottle of whiskey to Mzee on his birthday. My mother did that, always with some plausible excuse why he couldn't come himself.'

'Your father was too busy?'

'It wasn't about how busy he was. He didn't know or care about such things.' She'd never thought about it before, not consciously, and pushed her hair back from her face with her fingers, as if that would make everything clearer. 'He's never remembered my birthday since he didn't have Mom to prompt him to say happy birthday. There was no room in his head for anything but his work.'

'There was enough room for him to notice his assistant.'

'He'd been offered a new research project, more money, more prestige, and was ready to up sticks and leave. My mother refused to leave their work at Nymba unfinished, so he left her, taking a research student with him. Someone to deal with the tedious stuff of life. Organise food, make sure there were clean clothes, keep the records and type up the notes. And, I imagine, anything else he wanted.'

'I'm not your father, Eve.'

'No, you have more humanity in your little

finger than he has in his entire body, but sailing is your life, Kit. It has been since you could walk and to have achieved what you've done takes the kind of a single-minded focus that leaves no room for anything else.'

'That's why you asked me about the round-the-world race.'

'And you couldn't give me an answer.'

For a moment there was only the *tick-tick-tick* of the cooling engine and then Kit leaned forward, brought it back to life and drove on, barely slowing, even when an antelope burst through the bush and leapt across the track in front of them.

They parted awkwardly when they arrived back at the lodge.

'I'll book the first available flights,' he said, 'and let you know when we'll be leaving.'

She nodded.

'No arguments?'

'I want to be home, too.'

It was only when she was back in her suite that she remembered her promise to give Kit the photographs of Hannah.

She took out her phone, found a little video she'd taken of her putting together a puzzle.

Hannah was chattering to herself as she worked out how the pieces fitted together and then, when she'd finished, she clapped and looked up with that great big smile and said, 'I won!'

'Go to Daddy,' she whispered as she hit send, and a few moments later, the words 'I'm in love' came back.

The flight home was long and exhausting without the luxury of a break in London. Kit heard Eve give a sigh of relief as the lights of the harbour appeared out of the light sea mist and the ferry came into Nantucket.

Once they'd docked, he took her bag and headed for the taxi he'd called and, while the driver loaded her bag, asked, 'When can I see her?'

'It's late. She'll be in bed and first thing she'll only care about playing with her cousins. It will be more peaceful at the cottage.'

'When?'

'Come to lunch.'

'I'll bring it. What does she like?'

'Hannah loves a pizza. Just a simple one. Nothing spicy.'

'And what about you, Eve? I know you like pasta.'

'No...' Her blushes told him that she remembered how they had cooked it, how they had eaten it. One day, soon, they would do that again... 'A seafood pizza would be great. I'll make a salad.'

He opened the taxi door, watched her safely in and then closed it and stood back. She looked around as the car turned a corner and then was gone.

He hadn't told anyone he was coming home and he picked up his bag, slung it over his shoulder and began to walk. He'd just dropped his bag and fished out his keys when his phone pinged to let him know he had a message.

No words. Just a video of his daughter, stirring in her sleep, as if she sensed her mother's presence. He sat on the steps for a long time, playing it over and over, watching her breathe, watching Eve's hand as she smoothed back a curl and settled the comforter around their little girl.

'Martha? I'm sorry to call you so late—'
'Eve? Is anything wrong?'

'No. I'm home. I came back early.'

'Well, that's a shame. Wasn't the trip what you expected?'

'Oh, yes, absolutely. The lodge was lovely and I met so many people I hadn't seen since I was a child.'

'Including Hannah's father?'

'Martha—'

'I had lunch with his grandmother yesterday. She told me that Kit had gone out there for a meeting.'

'You knew?' Eve, who had retreated to the privacy of the veranda of Mary's home, sat down on the nearest chair.

'I guessed. Obviously something had happened to make you leave the way you did. You'd been to Laura Merchant's party and while either of the Merchant boys might have got lucky,' she said, 'what Brad was up to is a matter of public record.'

'Kit said she's the image of his sister as a child.'

'And that.'

'Why didn't you say anything?'

'You didn't want me to know, Eve, and I respected that.'

'I didn't want anyone to know,' she admitted, 'including Kit.'

'And now he does, I'm guessing. How does he feel about it?'

'He's furious with me for keeping her from him. He doesn't understand why I did that.'

'And what about you?' she asked. 'Do you know why?'

'I didn't. I was ashamed.' She sighed. 'I didn't want my mother gossiped about and Kit wasn't to blame—I threw myself at him.'

'He didn't drop you.'

'No, but I assumed he was well-practised. By the time I realised I was pregnant he was taking part in the round-the-world race. I saw his single-minded focus and thought he was like my father. I loved him, Martha, but he gives nothing back.'

'Your father is completely self-obsessed. Ridiculously good-looking, of course, and your mother was very young when she met him. A fatal attraction.'

'I still wish she was here.'

'But she wouldn't be. She loved you, Eve, but she wasn't cut out to sit at home and be a grandmother. She would be in Central America, or Africa or Asia.'

'I know, but I could call her, talk to her.'

'I know. It's hard but Kit isn't like your father. He may be single-minded, laser focussed in a way that few of us can imagine, but he dropped everything when his father had a stroke and came home.'

'And he hates it. He wants to get married and play happy families right now, but how long will it be before he's missing the adrenaline rush? Looking out to sea with that thousand-yard stare? I don't care for myself, Martha, but I want more than that for Hannah.'

'Would not being married to him be any different? You'd still be watching and waiting, feeling the fear, but think of the joy when he comes home.'

'You think I should marry him?'

'If you love him.'

'I barely know him.' She shook her head. 'I'm sorry to burden you with this, Martha, but I had to talk to someone. Maybe I was hoping that you would wave your magic godmother wand and somehow make it all go away.'

'No wand, I'm afraid, but for now it's all

about Kit and Hannah.' She gave a little sigh. 'There'll be media interest. It's going to be uncomfortable whatever you decide, but keep your mouth shut and a smile on your face and it will pass. I'm here for you. Whenever you need me.'

After more reassurances and a promise to call her after Kit's visit, Eve sat for a while, watching the video of her little girl sleeping, blissfully unaware that her young life was about to change for ever.

CHAPTER TWELVE

KIT WAS RIGHT. The cottage needed a lot more than a facelift and, shut up for a week, it was also stale and covered in dust.

There was nothing to be done about the heavy dark furniture and faded curtains, but Eve had set her alarm and, leaving Hannah sleeping at Mary's, went to open the windows to let the sea air blow through. She fed the cat, who seemed unusually pleased to see her, and then went to town with hot water, furniture polish and the vacuum cleaner.

Once she had the place shining, she dashed to the market to pick up groceries and flowers, collecting her daughter, and a casserole Mary pressed on her, on the way home.

'Thanks so much for having Hannah. I can't tell you how grateful I am.'

'She's a sweetheart. I'll have her any time. I'm just sorry you cut your trip short...' The unasked question hung in the air.

'It's a long story and you'll have it all, I promise, but I have to go. I'm expecting someone.'

'An agent?'

'No. I've decided to stay.'

'Well, that's the best news I've heard this week,' she said, enveloping her in a hug, 'and you can leave this little one with us any time. We're going to miss her,' she said, as they walked to the door. 'Oh, and the children were thrilled with their presents, by the way. You will get thank-you letters.'

'They weren't disappointed that I didn't bring them a real lion cub?'

'I explained that mummy lions get really cross if you try to take their babies away. And the stuffed ones don't scratch or harbour bitey insects. The bitey insects seemed to sway it.'

'Bitey things with too many legs can cause all kinds of problems,' Eve said, with feeling.

It was still shy of twelve when she reached the cottage but there was a dashing classic Morgan two-seater parked in her driveway.

It was exactly the kind of car that, if she had ever thought about it, she could imagine Kit driving and, as she parked her rental alongside it, she saw him sitting on the porch steps waiting for them.

She lifted Hannah from her car seat, set her down and opened the trunk.

'Do you want to give me a hand with these?' she said, holding out a bag when Kit hung back.

'I know I'm early,' he said, taking it from her, 'but I couldn't wait.'

'Of course you couldn't,' she said, climbing the steps, unlocking the door, conscious that Hannah, clinging to one hand, was craning her head to look back at Kit as he followed them. 'I'd have been here earlier, but I had to get groceries. Take those through to the kitchen.'

'Yes, ma'am.'

'Take off your shoes, and put them away, sweetie.'

'Yes, Mama.'

Aware that Kit was watching Hannah like a child at Christmas, she said, 'Do you want to put that stuff in the fridge, while I find a jug for the flowers?'

'Yes. Yes, of course.'

He put away milk, cheese, eggs, not taking his eyes off Hannah, who was making a meal out of taking off her shoes, well aware that she was the centre of attention.

'She's noticed you, Kit. Give her a minute and she'll be climbing all over you.'

'I'm torn between awe and terror.'

She smiled. 'That's about right.' She found a pair of scissors and began to snip the stalks off the daisies she'd bought. 'How's your dad?'

'Still struggling with words, making them up as he goes along, having to count from one until he gets to the number he wants, but he's stronger. Walking better.'

'That's good news. And is everyone happy with your Nymba trip?'

'I came back with a bunch of new ideas put forward by the trust. All I need now is for Brad to pull off something amazing so that I can get my life back.'

She stopped snipping. 'Why don't you try living the life you have, Kit?'

He stared at her for a moment, but then Hannah, used to being the centre of attention, was tugging at the leg of his jeans.

'I'm Hannah,' she said. 'Who are you?'

Kit, taken aback by such a direct approach, looked across at her for help.

'Tell her, Kit.'

'Straight out?'

She'd lain awake half the night trying to think of some way to explain who this strange man was to her little girl. Now he was here, it seemed the simplest thing in the world.

'Straight out,' she said, and watched as he folded himself up so that he was on a level with Hannah.

'I know who you are, Hannah Rose Merchant Bliss. I am Christopher Harrison Merchant.'

'We have the same name.'

'That's because I'm your daddy.'

Hannah frowned. 'My daddy isn't here.'

The pain was fleeting. If she hadn't been watching so closely, desperate to monitor both Hannah's and Kit's reaction to this momentous first meeting, she would have missed it.

'I'm here now, Hannah,' Kit said.

It was Hannah's turn to look to her, seeking confirmation. 'It's true, Hannah. Your daddy has been living a long way away from us, out on the sea, but now he's come home.'

'Where on the sea?'

'In a boat,' he said.

'Are we going to live on a boat with you?'

'Would you like that?'

Eve uttered a slightly strangled, 'No...'

But Hannah, seeing only the practicalities, said, 'It would be a bit small and Mungo wouldn't like it, but you could live here. We have lots of rooms. Do you want to see?'

'I think we should ask your mama if that's okay.'

Too late for that...

'You can show Daddy around the cottage, Hannah.'

'Okay. Well, this is the kitchen. It's big, but it needs work,' she said, parroting the realtor who'd come to give her opinion.

He stood up, looked around, then back at Hannah and, picking up on the language said, 'It has a lot of potential.'

Eve gave him a congratulatory smile as Hannah, satisfied with his answer, took his hand and led him to the sunroom.

'This is where I play when it rains,' she said, taking Kit's hand and pulling him into the enclosed sunroom on the back porch.

'You have a doll's house.'

'It was Nana's when she was a little girl.'

'It's very fine.'

Eve stood in the kitchen, putting the daisies, one by one, into a yellow jug, listening to the running commentary as Hannah gave Kit the grand tour.

'This is the living room. Mama says the carpet is...' She paused, trying to remember the word she'd used.

'Brown?' Kit suggested, helpfully. 'What colour do you think would look good in here?'

'Green. Like grass. With daisies.'

'Interesting. I like it.'

Eve swallowed down the lump in her throat. He was so good with her...

'This is the study. It's a nightmare.' Full stress on the word nightmare. 'There's stuff in here that should have been put on a bonfire years ago.'

Kit caught her eye as Hannah led him back across the hall. 'She's very...fluent.'

'I should have warned you. She was talking in sentences at eighteen months. Be careful what you say because it will come back to haunt you.'

'I'm getting that,' he said, clearly captivated.

He had yet to experience the kind of embarrassment bomb a small girl could drop when you least expected it, but she was glad that their first encounter was such a delight for both of them. And just a little bit terrified that he was going to steal her little girl's heart...

'Daddy!'

Eve pulled her lips back. Torn between laughter and tears. 'Pay attention, Daddy.'

Kit's poker face was history. He had the same, sandbagged look of raw love that she'd been wearing in the photographs her friends had taken when the newborn Hannah had been placed in her arms.

'The cloakroom is here,' Hannah said, 'but you don't want to see that.'

'I don't?'

'Mama is fixing it up, but she doesn't know what the heck she's doing. It's a mess.'

There you go, kiddo. Talk like that and your Merchant grandma is going to think I'm the world's worst mother. But she was laughing even as she wiped away a tear with the heel of her hand.

Hannah's voice, clear and carrying, continued to reach her as they went upstairs. 'This is Nana's bedroom. She died.'

'I'm sorry to hear that.'

'Did you know her?'

'I met her once,' he said. 'A long time ago when I was not much older than you.'

'Was she nice?'

'She gave me a cake. With icing.'

'She gave me her cottage,' Hannah said.

'Well, that's nice, too, but you can't eat a cottage.'

There was a moment of silence and Eve knew that Hannah would be frowning as she thought that through. Which was better, a cake or a cottage? A tricky decision when you were three years old. There would be questions later.

'I don't like it in here.'

'It's a bit gloomy,' he agreed.

'It's okay, Mama doesn't sleep in there.'

'Right.' He sounded bemused, but Eve was afraid she knew what was coming next and she didn't have to wait long.

'Cara and Jason and Lacey's mommy and daddy sleep in the same room, so you can share Mama's room.'

'It's very pretty.'

'The bathroom is an icky green but the other bathroom needs a plum.'

Eve covered her face with her hands. She really was going to have to start thinking before she opened her mouth. And never ever pass comment on other people's colour schemes.

'It's a bit early for plums. What colour is your bedroom, Hannah?'

'It's white, which is boring. Cara's daddy painted her bedroom pink. With a white trim.'

Eve didn't have to be in the room to know that she would be looking up at Kit with the sweetest smile. That child could work a room like an award-winning actress...

'Pink is lovely, but I think your pretty red hair needs a cool colour. Blue, maybe, to match your eyes. With a white trim,' he added when he didn't get immediate joy.

'Can I have a unicorn?'

'A real one?' he asked. 'Will there be room?'

Hannah giggled. 'Don't be silly. On the wall.'

'I think that could be arranged. And maybe a rainbow?'

Eve heard another delighted giggle.

'There is a room up some more stairs, but I'm not allowed to go up there.'

'Maybe your mama will show me later. Shall we go back down now? I need to order lunch and a little bird told me that you like pizza.'

'What little bird?'

'His name is Charlie. He lives on the beach.'

No...!

Kit had carried her downstairs and Hannah had her arms around his neck, looking straight into his eyes as she said, 'Can we go to the beach and look at your boat?'

'Lunch, then a nap, young lady,' Eve said, before he could answer.

Kit sat down, with her on his knee, and took out his phone, flipping through the menu, letting her look and guiding her choice.

'What shall we do until the pizzas arrive?' he asked.

'Can I play a game on your phone?'

'No, Hannah.'

Kit looked up, clearly about to say that she could do what the heck she liked with his phone, but thought better of it when he saw her *Don't you dare contradict me* face.

'Why don't you draw Daddy a picture?' she suggested.

'Of his boat?' She looked up at him and he obediently flipped through his phone until he found a picture of a small sailing dinghy.

Hannah drew the boat, then a family—mama,

daddy and a little girl with red hair all holding hands—with a house in the background and a very large sandcastle.

She could see that Kit was desperate to take it, keep it, but Hannah thought that, like her cousins' daddy, Kit would come home every day so was fixing it to the fridge with a magnet.

Hannah chattered happily through the pizza, telling Kit about everything she'd been doing for the last week until, having talked herself to a standstill, went down for a nap without protest.

When she was asleep they stood, awkwardly, in the kitchen.

'You were great with her,' Eve said.

'I don't know which feeling is strongest right now,' Kit said. 'Gratitude that I have such a beautiful child, or anger that I've missed so much.'

Which pretty much mirrored her own feelings. Gratitude that he had been so wonderful with Hannah, that he had adored her on sight. Anger that he didn't understand how his little girl would feel when he disappeared back to his real life.

'You would have been away six months of the year,' she reminded him, briskly. 'The sea is your first love and you can't wait to get back to it.'

'You think that excuses what you did?'

'No, but I think you should take a reality check. It's not all pizza and unicorns.'

'I know that.'

'Do you? Your life does not, will never, resemble the picture Hannah drew.'

'I'm not going anywhere,' he declared and she was sure that, as he said it, he believed it. 'How long will she sleep?'

'For about an hour.'

'In that case I have time to go and pick up some paint.'

'Paint?'

'Hannah thinks white is boring.'

'I heard, but you don't have to paint her room. I'll get around to it.'

'You have your hands full with the cloak-room.' He paused at the door. 'Thank you for last night. The video.'

'You're welcome. Forget about marriage and you can have all the highlights without the boring or messy bits. Never be the parent saying no.'

'I've got a better idea. You give me a list of the stuff you don't think she should be allowed so that we can discuss it. Just remember that I have a say in that.'

'No phone, no tablet, no computer games.'

'I saw your face when she asked about my boat.'

She desperately wanted to say *no boats* but this was Nantucket and Hannah's father was a world-famous sailor.

'I'm sorry. This is hard...'

He came back, put his arms around her and drew her to him. 'I'll follow your lead, Eve, but you're not on your own any more. From here on in it's the two of us.' He leaned back, looked down at her. 'I should have asked if you're happy with blue for her bedroom?'

She nodded, swallowed. 'Whatever makes Hannah happy.' She walked with him to the door, watched him drive away, then went back to the kitchen, took the picture down from the fridge and scanned it, putting the copy she'd printed out back on the fridge door. Then she opened up her laptop.

She had dozens of video clips of Hannah, from the moment of her birth until the one of her sleeping that she'd sent to Kit last night.

She couldn't give him back the time he'd lost, but she could give him a glimpse of some of those precious moments. And maybe one or two meltdown moments to remind him that it wasn't all unicorns and rainbows.

When Hannah saw the paint, she forgot all about boats. She wanted her room painted. Now.

'It's too late to start today, sweetheart,' Eve said. 'I'll have to move your bed.'

'Where do you want it?' Kit asked. 'She doesn't like Nana's room.'

'It's the big dark furniture and the smell of lavender polish. I didn't like it when I was little.' She pulled a face. 'To be honest, I don't like it now.'

'It's going to be a big bonfire.'

'I can't burn it! It's antique!' He grinned, she rolled her eyes, then laughed. The two of us, she realised, could be a lot more fun than do-it-yourself. 'You can take her bed into my room.'

The furniture moved, they were 'helped' by

Hannah as they took down the curtains and ripped up the old carpet.

Hannah had scrambled eggs and toast soldiers for tea. Eve and Kit had Mary's casserole. The icky green bathroom, and everyone in it, got soaked when Kit introduced water fountain play at bath time and then he read his little girl a bedtime story before, having tucked her in, he set to work on her bedroom.

'I'll bet you didn't think you'd be filling dints and cracks in the plaster this evening,' Eve said, as she set about rubbing down the paintwork.

'I've done a lot today that I never imagined. I'd stay later, but I promised to give Mom a break tonight.'

'You should go. I can handle this.'

'No. I've got until ten. It's just in case he wakes up and needs something, or someone. He likes to be read to.'

After a couple of hours they stopped for a cup of tea, sitting side by side on the floor, backs to the wall.

'When did you get so good at DIY?' Eve asked.

'The resort, obviously, was decorated to the highest standard, but Dad didn't believe in pay-ing union rates for the parts that were not on view. We were expected to pitch in and do what was needed in the offices, the storage units and outbuildings. Laura, too.'

'Equal opportunities child labour?'

'He said it was character-building. Maybe we should get Hannah painting tomorrow.'

'If you like, but you'll be in charge of cleaning up.'

'What about you?' he asked. 'It's not the first time you've sanded down a door.'

'When I moved into my mother's flat I was an eighteen-year-old student with a paintbrush and no one to stop me. I made a lot of mistakes—purple is not an easy colour to live with. The Internet taught me that preparation is all, and practice makes perfect.'

'But not, apparently, in the downstairs cloakroom.'

'It's my first attempt at tiling and the walls are not straight. I'm afraid I let my frustration show.'

'I've got a cure for that.'

Eve felt her cheeks grow hot.

'A spirit level?' he suggested, but his eyes

were saying something else and his mouth was within an inch of hers when Hannah cried out.

'It's the strange room,' she said, ridiculously flustered. 'I'll go and settle her.'

But Hannah wanted her daddy.

He tucked her in, gave her a kiss and said, 'See you tomorrow, honeybun,' and she was asleep again before he left the room.

'She wanted to be sure you were still here,' Eve said.

'And you? Do you want me to stay?'

'It doesn't matter what I want. I know you'll leave.'

'You don't think a man can change course?' He dug in his jeans pocket and produced a small velvet ring box. 'If you don't like this, you can choose something else, but it's my promise that I'll always be there for Hannah. For both of you.'

CHAPTER THIRTEEN

KIT TOOK THE ring from the box but, while she'd given an involuntary gasp at a stunning diamond, flanked by rubies, that lay tucked into the velvet, Eve instinctively drew back.

'My hands are dirty,' she said. 'My nails are chipped.'

'If you want to get yourself gussied up, I'll take you out to dinner and go down on one knee,' he offered.

Startled, she dragged her gaze from the mesmerising sparkle to his face. 'You have got to be kidding.'

'Am I laughing?'

'Don't even think about it.'

He shrugged. 'If you're sure.'

'Sure? Kit, this is crazy. We barely know one another. Not in any way that matters,' she added, before he said something outrageous. 'I promise you don't need a wedding band, or a court order, to see Hannah. That you want to

be a dad to her means more to me than I can
begin to say, and I swear on everything that I
hold dear that I will make our lives here. You
can see Hannah as often as you wish. Pick her
up from preschool, take her for ice cream, play
on the beach—'

'Teach her to sail?'

She barely hesitated before she said, 'Teach
her to sail. But marriage is a leap into the dark
and the landing can be painful.'

'We can have a prenup,' he said. 'I'd hate for
anyone to think I was after Hannah's cottage.'

'Oh, for heaven's sake…' Kit had made mil-
lions through sponsorship and endorsements.
He was the one who needed to guard his for-
tune. 'Can you be serious for a moment?'

'I have never been more serious in my life.'
His free hand was on her shoulder, the one
with the butterfly. 'We both know that if you'd
wanted money, you could have had it any time.
The lawyers might have insisted on a DNA test
but I would have known. You wouldn't have
had to go to court.'

'How could I have been so wrong about you?'

'You didn't know me.'

'Yes… Yes, I did.'

'And I know that your promise is everything.'

'And yet there is a but coming.'

'I'm sorry, but… You said I needed a dose of reality and this is as real as it gets. I want my daughter to have my name, Eve. Not hidden away where no one ever sees it,' he said, before she could speak, 'but on the school register. I want to be there at bedtime not just for the stories, but to make sure she brushes her teeth. To feel the panic when she has a fever. I don't want to be the parent who swoops in with gifts, trips to theme parks, a puppy.'

'No puppy!'

'If I was an irresponsible father, with no conscience, I would put one in her arms and you wouldn't be able to do a thing about it.'

'But you're not and you wouldn't,' she said.

'I don't want to the part-time parent who is all about outings, toys, but never there when she's kicking off and being a brat.'

'You will so regret saying that when she's five going on fifteen.'

'I have a sister and, believe me, I have no illusions.'

'Seriously?'

'I don't want to be there just for the good

stuff, I want to be there for all the stuff, and for that to happen, Eve, I need you. I checked the resort bookings this morning and there's space next Wednesday.'

He wasn't saying, I love you, will you marry me?

No pretence, no romance but she wouldn't have believed him if he had.

He was saying, I need you, you will marry me.

It wasn't romantic, but it was honest. And she hadn't said no. She'd said her hands were dirty and he believed he'd won.

'That's less than a week.'

'You were the one who mentioned the Las Vegas option.'

'I wasn't serious! I understand how you feel, Kit, but you've been hit by an emotional bombshell,' she said. 'You're not thinking rationally. Give it some time and you'll see I'm right.'

'Is there someone else?' he asked.

'What? No. No!' she repeated. 'There has never been anyone else since that night.'

'No one? You were never lonely?'

'I've steered clear of beaches since the night we made Hannah, Kit. She takes all my time.'

'I doubt you'll believe me but there has been no one else for me, either.' He put his head back against the wall, looking up at the ceiling, but she didn't think he was seeing much, except emptiness.

'No one?' she asked, with the same intensity as he'd asked that question.

'There were plenty of opportunities,' he admitted, 'but when you looked at me it was as if no one had ever seen me before. I searched for you all that summer, Eve, and since then, wherever in the world I was, I have turned at the sight of every redhead.' He grinned. 'Which was beginning to get embarrassing. But I never stopped looking, and that night at the auction… I didn't know you were there, but I felt something. You had marked me on your skin, Eve, and that night I caught the scent of vanilla and the air shimmered.' He was still holding her hand and this time she didn't pull back, allowing him to slip the ring onto her finger.

For a moment she was mesmerised by the rainbow flash of the diamond against her gritty hand and all she could think was that she really should have washed it first.

'Rubies? For a redhead?'

'The jeweller suggested emeralds but they seemed so cold. Rubies match your warmth, Eve, but if you'd prefer—'

'No. It's a bold choice, Kit. I love them.'

'You will always be Red to me. I have carried the scent of vanilla with me, carried you with me wherever I was in the world.'

'What...? How could you do that? You didn't know who I was.'

He reached for the battered leather backpack he always carried over one shoulder and from its depths he produced a small grey velvet elephant.

Its back and head were faded and, where it had been held by small fingers, hugged in sleep, the lush velvet pile was rubbed away, but there were still places in the folds where the legs met the body and where, hidden from the light, you still could feel the richness of the fabric.

'Ellie...' She breathed the word.

She looked so small in Kit's large, callused hands, but as she reached out, not quite able to believe her eyes, he placed the toy in her hands and she carried her to her cheek, her eyes closed, remembering the moment her mother had given the elephant to her.

'Where did you find her?' she asked.

'On the beach. It must have fallen out of your bag. Your Cinderella moment. It's not a glass slipper, but then I doubt a glass slipper would have survived what this little elephant has been through.'

'Not something you'd hug,' she admitted. 'But she's so worn, not even good enough to donate to Goodwill. Most men would have tossed her into the nearest bin.'

'She has the look of something long loved and I carried her with me all that summer so that when I found you, I could give it to you.'

Because he was not most men. She'd felt how special he was when he'd come to sit with her on the beach because she looked lost and un-happy…

'I only realised she was gone when I was in the departure lounge at the airport,' she said. 'It felt as if my mother had reached out from beyond the grave, so disappointed in me that she'd taken her back…'

'No!' He put his arms around her, drew her close. 'No. If she did anything, she plucked it out of your bag, leaving it for me to find. It wasn't a glass slipper, but it was all I had.'

With her face buried in his shoulder, the steady thud of his heartbeat bringing her own back down until it was riding in tandem with his, smothered in the scent of his body, his clothes, she knew that this was just comfort.

The beach all over again.

But she clung on long after the threatened tears had evaporated, as long as she could without making a fool of herself.

Eventually, though, she drew back. 'Sorry. I...' She shook her head. 'It's just a shabby toy. I can't believe you've kept it all this time.'

'A fairy-tale prince would have carried that glass shoe with him and never stopped looking until he found the girl the shoe fitted.'

'By which time he would have a long white beard and she would be a wrinkled old crone. Real fairy tales tend to have a bitter twist to them,' she said, but she was laughing. 'Thankfully, you are no Prince Charming.'

'And you are no Cinderella. But your Ellie and I have become very close.'

'You really have carried her with you?'

'The early settlers in the west kept a grab-

and-run bag by the door. Each night they'd put in their family Bible, the spindle from their spinning wheel, those things that were precious to them, that couldn't be replaced. Then they hung it on the door handle, ready to grab if there was fire, or an attack and they had to run for their lives and start again.'

'And…'

'This is my grab-and-run bag,' he said. 'The one that would go into the life raft with me if I had to abandon ship. It has been home to your little elephant since the day you left. She sailed around the world with me and we have kept each other safe.'

Eve held Ellie against her face for a moment, breathing in the scent of leather, the sea, the vanilla scent that her mother wore. Then she offered it back to him.

'Keep her. We all need something, someone to keep us safe. She is your mascot and my promise to you that wherever you go, Hannah will be here when you return.'

'But—'

'She is no longer lost and neither am I.'

He took it and, holding it in one hand, he

reached out and cradled her cheek with the other.

'And you, Eve? Will you be here?'

For a moment he waited, not forcing it, waiting for her to come to him. Just one kiss. She wanted it so much, and they were so close that she could feel the heat of his mouth. She leaned her cheek into his hand, closed her eyes...

'Mama!'

His hand slipped to the nape of her neck and he rested his forehead against hers. 'You are never alone with a child,' she said, a little shakily. Then she drew back a little, kissed his forehead and went to see what Hannah wanted.

Kit leaned his head back against the wall. Nearly. So very nearly, but, despite her initial resistance, she was not only wearing his ring but had given him her own most precious possession. And they had been a breath away from a kiss. And not just any kiss. *The* kiss.

Today he had a daughter and a promise.

Tomorrow anything could happen.

'Have you told your family?'

'About Hannah?' Kit shook his head. They

were standing on the porch, he had to go, but he'd never wanted to stay anywhere so desperately in all his life.

They'd had so little time and soon the world would crash in on them. He'd hoped that they would have been able to just sit and be together for a while. A few days, a week maybe, but he'd blown it.

'I thought we needed a little time before we had to face my family, but this afternoon I walked into a jeweller's in broad daylight.'

'On a small island like Nantucket? What on earth were you thinking?'

Eve was shaking her head, but smiling, and he took her hand, looked at the ring he'd placed on her finger. She'd taken it off to scrub away the dust, but she had put it back on.

'The truth, Eve? I haven't been thinking since you walked into the lodge with Peter Ngei and everything I'd been feeling since that morning made sense.'

'I…' She swallowed, for a moment floundering for a response. 'I've told my godmother, Martha Adams, that you are Hannah's father,' she said. 'I didn't want her to hear it as gossip.'

'I'm glad you did. I've known Martha all my life. She's a friend of my grandmother.'

'She won't say anything, but she had already guessed. And your car has been parked here all day in full view of anyone passing. I doubt there's another like it on the island.'

'I haven't exactly been discreet.'

'You never meant to be,' she said. 'You don't have to be.'

'So tomorrow, when I buy a family car with a state-of-the-art child seat, and the news is all over social media before the ink is dry on the receipt, you won't mind?'

'Your family need to know before your mother starts getting phone calls,' she said. 'And there are some people I have to tell before it becomes island gossip. The sooner the better.'

'Now?' He produced a phone from his pocket but she covered it with her hand.

'Face-to-face.'

'And the wedding? I know it's short notice, but we have someone who organises everything. I'll get her to call you—'

'Short notice? It's crazy. Your family will

think you've lost your mind. Or that I've got your arm twisted up behind your back.'

'You could try.'

'Metaphorically.'

'No one forced me to do anything in my entire life, metaphorically or otherwise, but Nana's room doesn't scare me. If you're going to insist on a long engagement, I can move in tomorrow.'

'What? No!'

'Then stop playing hard to get, Eve, or I'll start demonstrating just how much I remember about you. So if you don't want to disturb the neighbours...' She gave an involuntary shiver, backing into the post supporting the porch roof. 'So easy,' he said, following her.

'It's just sex...' Her voice was no more than a hoarse whisper as his fingers slid into her hair.

'I know.' His kiss was teasing, a slow touch-and-go that had her treacherous body crumbling against him, demanding more, but he was the one playing hard to get, his lips barely touching hers, his body a tormenting distance. 'Fun, isn't it?'

Her only response was a low, desperate rumble in the back of her throat and for a moment he was with her, fingers tangled in her hair, his own raw need matching hers, lost in the depths of a shattering kiss that answered every midnight dream.

They were both breathing heavily when he drew back.

'Marry me, Eve. Once you have my ring on your finger, you can have all the fun you want.'

'Marriage is more than sex.' A final bid for common sense.

'It's a good start and we have a lifetime to work on the rest.' He stepped back, putting clear air between them. 'Be prepared to have my mother on your doorstep first thing tomorrow.'

'No.'

And beyond the teasing, she saw a flash of anguish as he raked his hand back through his hair. She still had her doubts but Martha had said this was 'meant'.

'Your father should be there, too,' she said, 'and since he can't come to us right now, Hannah and I will come to you.'

'You are...' He shook his head and this time when he took her in his arms it was some-

thing else, his kiss all tenderness. Gratitude.
'I should go.'

'Kit...'

Eve took a pen drive from her pocket. 'This is yours.'

'What is it?'

'A memory stick.' She leaned forward, kissed his cheek then stepped back inside and closed the door before she did something really stupid, like begging him to stay.

She leaned back on the door, holding her breath until she heard him cross the gravel, not moving until the sound of his engine was just an echo in her head.

CHAPTER FOURTEEN

KIT HAD SAT with his family that morning and told them about Eve and Hannah. His mother had wept, Laura had whooped, his father had been unreadable.

Afterwards Brad had sought him out.

'So that's where you were the night I was arrested,' he said. 'Making babies with Eve.'

'I'm sorry, Brad. I let you down.'

'We both know I let myself down, Kit, but it's easier to blame someone else. I'm glad you found her and your little girl.'

For an awkward moment they just looked at one another, then they were hugging.

'Hey, I'm an uncle,' Brad said. 'Can I tell Lucy?'

'You like her? I mean really like her?'

'Yes, I do. She's a woman you can talk to. Are you really going to set up a boat design business with her?'

'Have you a problem with that?'

'Not if it means she'll be staying here.'

'Just…'

'I'm not messing, Kit…'

His voice trailed away as a car pulled into the drive. Eve climbed out and lifted Hannah from her car seat and she reached out to him.

'Daddy!'

He took her from Eve. 'Do you want to meet your Uncle Brad?' he asked.

She looked over his shoulder and then back at him. 'Okay.'

'Eve, meet the brains of the family.'

'Hello, Brad,' she said, offering her hand.

He held it, shaking his head. 'My brother is one lucky man. As for you, young lady…' he said, turning to Hannah. 'Laura, but with red hair. You are going to be so much trouble.'

He'd imagined a slightly stiff meeting in the drawing room with his mother, but she was down the porch steps with Laura at her heels, stopping short, a hand to her mouth as she saw Hannah.

'Hannah Rose…' She took one little hand and held it for a moment while they looked at one another. 'You and I are going to have so much fun.' Then she smiled at Eve. 'Hello, Eve, I'm

Barb and this is Laura, who is going to disappear right now so that we can get to know one another.'

'Don't worry,' Laura said. 'Mom isn't going to grill you. She's thrilled because it means Kit will be staying. Can I be a bridesmaid?' She didn't wait for Eve to answer before turning to him. 'Who is going to be your best man, Kit?'

'Brad,' he said.

She pulled a face. 'Well, that's no fun.'

'Kit,' his mother said, 'your father is on the deck waiting to meet his granddaughter.'

He took Eve's hand, kissed her cheek before turning to his mother. 'Do not show her baby photographs.'

His father was sitting on the deck, a rug around his knees. His mother had searched out some of the wooden puzzles that they'd had as kids to help his father and there was one on a small table at his side.

Kit put Hannah down and knelt beside her. 'This was my puzzle when I was little,' he said. 'Grandpa's hands aren't working very well at the moment. Do you think you could help him put the pieces in the right place?'

Hannah looked up at his dad, picked up a

piece and showed it to him. 'The chicken goes here...'

They both watched her for a moment as she slotted the farmyard animals into place and then his dad looked up at him and he smiled.

'Your family were so kind to me, Kit,' Eve said later, when they took Hannah home for a nap after a family lunch. 'And you were such a cute baby.'

He groaned, but was grinning. 'Hannah and Dad were great together. She chatted to him the way she does, and he was so gentle with her. He managed to say Han, and when he put all the pieces in the puzzle she clapped.'

'She's had a lot to take in, but you've all given her space, let her take the lead, so she hasn't felt overwhelmed.'

'She is adorable. We are all at her feet. You have done an amazing job, Eve. Dad smiled at me for the first time in years and when I took his hand, he squeezed it.'

'That's wonderful. I'm so happy for you.'

'There are no words.' He took her hands. 'I swear I will do everything I can to make you happy, Eve.'

She lifted a hand to his face, feeling the soft-
ness of his beard against her palm for a moment. 'Marriage is a partnership, Kit. We both
have to work at it.'

'I can take a hint. I found some overalls—'

He stopped as she raised herself on her toes
and touched her lips to his.

'Just working on it,' she said and then, because he didn't seem to know what to do next,
'Are you okay about living here?'

There was a plaintive *miaow* as Mungo,
emerging from his hiding place in the airing
cupboard, curled himself around Kit's legs.

'That cat votes stay,' he said, and was rewarded with a purr when he bent to stroke him.

'Even with the icky green bathroom?' Eve
said.

'It's nothing a coat of paint won't fix.' He
looked up. 'When Hannah's had her nap we
could go to the hardware store and pick out a
colour.'

'A deep pink would match the rosebuds on
the bedroom wallpaper.'

'About the flowers...'

'You're not keen?' She grinned. 'Better look
at wallpaper samples, too. In fact, it might be

easier to start at the top and work down. Do you want the top floor as a studio space? It's going to take a while to custom-build from scratch.'

'Eve...'

'Still working on it,' she said.

'Can I join in?'

'Help yourself,' she said, then felt her cheeks heat up as he grinned.

'I was going to suggest that while we're out we could call in at a dealership and choose a family car.'

The next day, Eve and Kit sat for a photograph that was issued by his agent with the announcement that Kit Merchant and Eve Bliss, who had a three-year-old daughter, were getting married in a private ceremony at the Merchant Resort in Nantucket. The media picked up on the fact he'd resigned as skipper for the racing season because his father had been seriously ill and connected the two events.

Lifestyle magazines immediately offered a seven-figure sum for the exclusive rights to cover the wedding.

Eve was horrified at the thought, but said, 'The money could go to the opioid clinic.'

'That is generous of you, but I'll donate the money myself before submitting my family and friends to that kind of intrusion.' He took out his phone and then looked at her. 'Are you okay with that?'

'Me?'

'I'm setting up a trust for Hannah, but if we're donating a million dollars to mark our wedding, you have a say.'

'I am lost for words.'

He grinned. 'I'll remember that if you ever get naggy.'

Kit might have imagined something small for the ceremony, but his mother and sister had other ideas. Fortunately, the Merchant wedding planner had everything under control. All Eve had to do was say yes.

Invitations were dispatched to Nymba, to the group who'd supported Eve at Hannah's birth, their family and Kit's friends who were coming from all over the world.

Laura and Lucy were both to be bridesmaids,

along with Hannah and her cousins; Jason, bless his heart, flatly refused to be a page boy.

All she had to do was choose a dress and she had Martha, Mary and Hannah eager to help her with that.

It seemed as if everyone was giving the pair of them time to get to know one another. Kit worked on Hannah's room in the morning while Eve went shopping, or took her to see her grandparents, or to play with Mary's children.

They had lunch together and after Hannah's nap they spent the afternoon on the beach, or in the pool at the resort, where Hannah's early swimming lessons proved their worth.

'She's a little fish,' Laura said. 'She should join Lucy's Puddleduck sailing class.'

Eve stiffened. Hannah had been desperate to get on a boat since that first day, drew pictures of them all the time, but as she hesitated, Kit said, 'Why don't I take both of you out? You'll be able to see for yourself if she enjoys it.'

She knew she was being selfish, that sailing was part of life on the island, in the Merchant blood, but she didn't want Hannah to enjoy it.

Kit was waiting, not pushing her, but this was

about learning to trust. For three years she'd had sole responsibility for this little bundle of joy and each small surrender was terrifying.

The first time she'd left him alone with Hannah was when she went shopping for a wedding dress. The first time she'd watched him drive away with her, just the two of them going for an ice cream. The first time he'd been the one she'd run to...

'I've never been in a sailing boat,' she said. 'I'd just be a liability. Hannah will let you know soon enough if she doesn't like it.'

Afterwards, when Hannah was in bed and they were alone, he said, 'The sailing thing. I know how hard that was for you.'

She shook her head. 'Maybe, when she's going out on her first date, you'll have some idea.'

'She is never going out on a date,' he said, then put his arms around her and drew her close, holding her as if he'd never let go. 'I'll take care of her, Eve.'

'I know you will.' She nodded. 'Nothing in the world will stop me from worrying until you're safely back on shore, but Hannah is as much yours as mine.'

'I'm scared witless by the responsibility.'

'Welcome to the club.'

'Thank you.' He brushed the curls back off her forehead. 'Now, on the subject of dates, I've been thinking that we should try that.'

'Dating?'

'Dinner somewhere. Or maybe there's something you'd enjoy at the arts centre?'

'You want to hold hands in the back row at a movie?'

'It's been a while but I'm sure I remember how that goes. We can have dinner afterwards.'

'I'll have to organise a babysitter.'

'Say the word and you'll be fighting them off. I'll check what's on.' His phone rang as he took it from his pocket. He glanced to see who was calling and then sent it to voicemail.

'You could have answered that.'

'It's nothing that won't wait. Okay, here we are,' he said. 'It's a live screening from the Met tomorrow. Opera?'

'Let's just have dinner. If you want to hold hands you can walk me home along the beach.'

'Tomorrow?'

'Tomorrow. Why don't you ask your mom if Hannah can have a sleepover?'

'You are a peach, but she'll think I'll be staying over.'

'Kit, she'll be babysitting our daughter so I don't imagine she'd be shocked, but if you think your macho reputation will be ruined if you go home, you are welcome to Nana's room. However, I'm sure Hannah would be thrilled to have you there when she wakes up.'

Cloud had blown in and there was rain in the air so they missed out the beach, but dinner overlooking the harbour had been lovely.

The food was doubtless perfect, but they'd talked so much that they'd scarcely noticed it. Even when Kit's phone had rung, he'd turned it off without even looking to see who had called.

He'd talked about his family, about being alone on the ocean, about his last holiday in France with Matt.

She had talked about her mother, about the kids she'd taught, about the chance of a prestigious job that she'd had to let go when her grandmother died.

'If she'd recovered,' he said, 'I would never have found you.'

'I would have found you,' she said. 'Hannah would have insisted.'

'Would it bother you if I said I would have liked you to have found me for you?'

'Maybe I'd been waiting for the excuse.'

Kit drove her home and walked her to her door. He took the keys from her, unlocked the door and Mungo strolled over and rubbed against Kit's legs.

'He likes you,' she said.

'He may change his mind when I bring home that puppy.' He looked up. 'No objections?'

'I've never had a dog.'

'We'll choose it together. Something with a soft mouth.'

She nodded. 'Are you coming in for coffee?'

'If I come in, I'll stay and I don't think you're ready for that. But I'll take a kiss.'

And he kissed her on the doorstep just as if it were an old-fashioned girl/boy date with her dad waiting on the other side of the door. Breathtakingly sweet and leaving her desperate for more.

* * *

The sea was quiet with the slightest breeze. It was very early when Kit took Hannah down to the dock before anyone was about.

Eve, having given him her trust, would have been on edge, transferring her nerves to their little girl.

He wanted her to experience that same thrill that he'd felt when his grandfather had taken him on the water for the first time. To have that same never to be forgotten moment of shared joy.

She was glowing with excitement as he smoothed sunblock on her face and hands, fitted her with a life jacket, talking her through what they were going to do, stressing on her the importance of listening to him and doing exactly what he said.

Half an hour later, as he brought the boat into the dock, Eve was standing on the dock, waiting for them.

She looked white, and when he lifted Hannah out of the boat and she ran to her exclaiming with excitement, she picked her up, kissed her.

'Did you enjoy that?' she asked, her voice

perfectly calm, but she turned her back on him, walking away.

He lowered the sail, tidied everything away and went to face her wrath.

She was waiting on a bench and he sat beside her. 'I didn't expect you until after breakfast.'

'I found Hannah's toothbrush.'

'Bad timing.'

'No.' He saw her swallow and then she reached out and grabbed his hand. 'I'll be fine, just give me a minute.'

'The rest of my life.'

She leaned against him and he put his arm around her. 'My red hair, your seafarer's genes.'

'Our little girl. Where is she, by the way?'

'Gone to tell her grandpa how she's going to be a sailor like her daddy.'

CHAPTER FIFTEEN

LUCY SIGHED. 'You look stunning, Eve.'

The mirror reflected the image of a bride. Still, solemn, her hand against the scalloped lace necklace that settled just below her collarbone, the rubies on the ring Kit had given her a deeper shade of red than her hair.

'Mom said it's as if Kit had a piece missing for the last few years,' Laura said. 'Now he's found you and he's complete.'

Except they all knew he wasn't.

He had closed his phone half a dozen times when she'd walked into a room, as guilty as if he'd been texting with a secret lover and, in a way, he was.

Finally, she'd called him on it.

'You don't have to hide it from me, Kit. It's natural to want to know what's happening with your team. When do the yacht trials begin?'

'Next week.' He'd looked back at the screen. 'The weather is a concern.'

'They won't go out in bad weather, surely?'

'We're— They're behind. The keel wasn't performing as well as we'd hoped. I'd suggested adjustments to the design, but it hadn't been tested.'

'You should be there.'

'I'm needed here.'

There had been nothing she could say that wasn't a cliché; she'd just rested a hand on his arm.

'I don't suppose cake tasting would take your mind off it?'

He had covered his hand with her own, acknowledging her concern, but had said, 'Could you and Hannah handle that? The new carpet is coming for her room tomorrow and there's still stuff to finish up here. Unless you want to spend your wedding night in Nana's room?'

He'd been kidding—they would be spending the night at one of the resort guest cottages— but his eyebrow, lifted in a way that suggested all kinds of pleasure, hadn't convinced.

He was worried. Not about her or Hannah or his family, but about his yacht and his crew.

* * *

The wedding ceremony took place in a gauzy pergola sparkling with fairy lights. Hannah, Cara and Lacey led the way, sprinkling rose petals in her path.

Hannah, until this moment the centre of attention, looked up at Kit, expecting him to pick her up, tell her how clever she was, how pretty she looked, but Laura and Lucy shepherded the girls into their seats and then it was just the two of them. Kit looking at Eve as she walked on her own towards him. Given away by no one. Giving herself with a whole heart and a clear head.

He smiled as she reached him and, once she'd handed her bouquet to Lucy, took her hand, mouthing a silent *Thank you*. Not the usual greeting of a groom to his bride, but she knew his mind was elsewhere.

The sunset ceremony was simple, their vows the old, traditional ones in which Christopher Harrison Merchant and Genevieve Bliss promised before witnesses to love, comfort and honour one another for as long as they both should live.

Maybe they should have thought that through,

written promises that avoided that dangerous four-letter word. Too late now, but it was debatable which of their hands was shaking the most as they exchanged rings.

Kit, unusually clumsy, fumbled the moment when he slipped the plain gold band on her finger. Aware that it was badly done, he looked up and said, 'This is scarier than a force nine gale...' raising a laugh from their guests, and then lifted her hand to kiss it and there was an audible sigh.

Eve slipped the second ring on his finger and then took his hand and was still holding it as the minister pronounced them man and wife and invited Kit to kiss his bride.

He took her face in his hands and murmured something, but his words were lost in the mayhem of clapping as his lips touched hers.

Later, after they had cut the cake, kissed and been kissed by all their family and friends, Kit took her hand.

'Will you dance, Mrs Merchant?'

She hadn't thought about a first dance; the incredibly efficient woman who had planned the whole thing hadn't mentioned it. As she hesitated, a guitarist began to pick out a familiar melody and, as Kit took her in his arms, the man began to sing.

'How did you know that I love this song?' she said, laying her head on his shoulder as, oblivious to those who had formed a circle around them, they stood, holding one another, barely moving.

'I've been working to your playlist as I decorated Hannah's room and the words were so perfect. The first time I saw you, kissed you, felt your heart beat…' The music had finished and they were standing, looking at one another, but then Hannah raced over to them and Kit bent to pick her up.

'Hello,' he said. 'Who is this little princess?'

She giggled, then said, 'Uncle Brad says that Mama has to throw her flowers away. Right now.'

Kit looked at her and grinned. 'How good is your aim?'

'I will do my best.'

With her bouquet safely caught by a blushing Lucy, Eve placed her tiara on Hannah's head, told her to be good for Grandma, then kicked off her shoes, carrying them, her lace hem trailing in the sand as they walked along the beach to the guest cottage.

The stars were thick and bright over the sea. 'Sailors used to navigate by the stars,' Eve said. 'Can you do that?'

'Second star on the right and straight on until morning.'

'That's the way to Neverland,' she said, and shivered, as if a goose had walked over her grave.

'Hey, kidding. You do know that we use GPS these days?'

'But suppose it broke down? No radio, no satellite tracking device, far out in the ocean, out of sight of land. You would be back in the Dark Ages.'

'Fifteenth-century sailors travelled the globe,' he reminded her. 'Drake, Vasco da Gama... And you might have heard of an Italian guy called Columbus?'

'I'm being serious.'

'I'm sorry. I do know how to use a sextant,' he assured her. 'I could bring us home using the sun and the stars...' He stopped, looking south, for a moment lost to her but then the breeze whipped at her dress, bringing him back to her. 'Why did you want to know?'

'Just checking,' she said, as they moved on.

The veranda of the guest house was lit by candles in elegant glass jars. There was champagne in an ice bucket and the scent from a bank of creamy roses, mingled with the sea air.

Kit picked up the glasses and champagne bottle, holding them in one hand. The other he kept for her, leading her along the candlelit path to the bedroom.

'Did I tell you that you look beautiful, Eve?'

'Um, let me think...'

'You look so lovely in that dress that I can only think of one way in which you would look even more beautiful.'

'And how is that?'

'Turn around and I'll show you.' She turned. 'Lift your hair...'

She swept her hair up with one hand and he began to unfasten the hooks that held the lace together, kissing her nape and every exposed inch of her spine.

Hooks done, he took his time lowering the zip, continuing his kissing game, unclipping her bra when it impeded his progress, until the dress slid with a gentle sigh to the floor.

Kit stirred. Eve was sleeping, her face in the pillow, her hair a wild red tangle of curls across the pillow. For a moment he watched her; in a while he would wake her but even as he thought about how he would do that an alarm sounded, not on his phone, but on hers.

'You put in an alarm call?' he asked, grinning.

'I did and it's time you were up and in the shower.'

'If that's an invitation—'

'No. It's a fact.' She rolled out of bed, tugged on a robe and headed for the kitchen. 'I'll get the coffee on.'

'Hey. Don't I get to sleep in on my honeymoon?'

'No, you get a helicopter out of here in just under half an hour. You have a plane to catch.'

'What?'

'Lucy told me that the team director has been calling you repeatedly. That, despite the fact that you want more than anything to be with them, you've been saying no.'

'She shouldn't have done that. She knows I can't go. The wedding, Hannah, Dad—'

'The wedding is cake crumbs, Hannah has a whole new family, and Brad and I talked to your dad. He knows this is your life, Kit, and so do I. He was scared he'd die and you wouldn't be here, but you came when you were needed and he knows now that you'll come back, spend more time here.'

'I'll stay as long as he needs me.'

'I really hope it was true when you said you didn't want to sit behind a desk running a resort complex because he's going to name Brad CEO today. Not acting. The whole deal. You are free.'

'Once you have a child, freedom becomes an irrelevance.'

'I know that Hannah will bring you back like a bungee rope, but it's not a chain, Kit. Live the life you have. It's my wedding gift to you.'

'I don't know what to say.'

'You don't have time for speeches. Travel clothes are in the wardrobe. Your bag is packed. Your flight is booked, so get in the shower while I fix your breakfast.'

Ten minutes later his ride landed on the resort's helicopter pad and as he appeared, hair still wet from the shower, Eve put a travel mug of coffee in his hand and tucked a pastry into his jacket pocket.

'I'll call you when I get there,' he said, pausing for one last kiss before picking up the bag with his sailing clothes and the battered leather backpack that were waiting by the door. 'Tell Hannah I love her.'

Eve stood on the veranda, waiting for the helicopter to take off, watching until he was no more than a black spot in the sky heading towards the mainland, then she took a deep breath in and sat on the kitchen stool, clutching a mug of coffee.

She wouldn't cry. Tears never changed a thing.

It was what it was.

She was doing pretty well until her phone rang. She checked the caller and saw that it was her fellow conspirator.

'Hi, Lucy.'

'I saw the helicopter take off. Do you need company?'

'I'm going to pick up Hannah later and take her to the beach. I know Brad will be super busy, so if you'd like to join us, you're welcome.'

'That would be fun, although I was wondering how you feel about sailing lessons.'

'For me? Is that Kit's idea?'

'No, but it might help you deal with the fact that Hannah is daddy's little girl and it will give you something other than a missing bridegroom to think about.'

'I... Can you teach me how to use a sextant?'

'Kit is the expert,' she said, 'but I can explain the basics.'

Kit drank the coffee Eve had made for him, ate the pastry, still not quite believing that he was on his way to Australia. That her heart was that big...

Just this once, he told himself. Just this once and he would go home, be a husband, a dad, a son. For now, his entire focus had to be on the race.

It was going to be a long day, a long flight. It was now Saturday in Sydney, around three in the afternoon, and he was already texting the chief engineer for an update. For the first time in his life, though, sailing wasn't his entire life, and while his head was fully engaged, his heart was lagging far behind.

His phone still in his hand, he texted Eve.

I can't believe how lucky I am. Or how stupid I am. I had a gift for you but I was distracted. You'll find it in the pocket of my tux. x

The beep of an incoming message roused Eve. The words shimmered for a moment.

Lucky.

An adjective to join 'thank you' in the pantheon of the world's most underwhelming words from a lover...

She put down the mug, went into the bedroom and picked up their discarded clothes. She checked Kit's pockets, finding his keys and a package beautifully wrapped in red tissue paper and tied with gold ribbon.

She put them to one side, folded his tux and her dress to take to the dry cleaner, putting the rest of their clothes aside for the laundry.

The keys she tucked in the handbag that had been delivered, along with a change of clothes, to the cottage the previous day. The package she carried through to the kitchen, holding it to her, not sure what Kit would have thought appropriate. Afraid that whatever it was would be saying *Thank you* and *I'm lucky...*

She was still sitting there when Lucy tapped on the door. 'Eve? Can I come in? You sounded a bit...' She gave an awkward little shrug. 'I thought a warm pastry might help. There's buttered, chocolate, almond—oh, love...' she exclaimed, dropping the bag on the counter and scooping Eve into her arms. 'He'll be okay,' she said as Eve's tears soaked into her T-shirt. 'He'll be back in no time.'

A month...

It would be a month. She'd known that and had told herself she was fine with it.

'I'm so sorry. I promised myself I wouldn't cry but it was the almond croissant. So stupid.'

'No. It's the little things that get you.'

'I'm sorry, Lucy. After all you've been through, you must think me totally pathetic.'

'No. I think, we all think, that you are amazing.'

Lucy made coffee, chatting brightly, giving her a moment to pull herself together. 'It was such a lovely wedding, Eve. Your dress was stunning and I nearly died when Kit kissed your hand. I've never seen anything so romantic, except maybe the look in his eyes in that moment when he said, "I love you…"'

'What?'

'Sorry. It was a totally private moment, but it can be so noisy on board that you get really good at lip-reading.'

That was what he'd said before he'd kissed her? I love you?

'I…um…do you mind, Lucy? I need to take a shower, get dressed.'

'Sure. I was just, you know…' She bent and picked up Kit's present. 'You must have dropped this when I grabbed you for a hug. Red? Unusual for a bride gift.'

'Kit called me Red the very first time he spoke to me.'

'I can't think why,' Lucy said, grinning as she headed for the door. 'See you later.'

Eve held the package for a moment, then pulled the ribbon, tore off the tissue paper. Inside was a square velvet box, too big for a pendant, maybe a watch…? Which would be totally weird.

Not a watch, but a bracelet. A very simple open coil of gold like nothing she'd ever seen, and beautiful in its own right. But on the inside was inscribed the first verse of the song written by Ewan MacColl for the woman he loved. The song about all those special first times. The song that Kit had arranged for them to dance to at their wedding.

She took her phone, heart in her hands as she wrote,

Come home safe, Kit Merchant. There's something I have to tell you.

Kit didn't miss his phone until he reached to put it in the tray, along with his laptop, belt and wallet, at airport security.

There was no time to go back and look for it. His flight had already been called and he barely had time to pick up a new pay-as-you-go in duty free. As soon as he was on board he called Brad and asked him to text him Eve's number.

'You don't know it?'

'My phone knows it,' he said.

'Oh, boy. Talk about husband fail.'

'Just—'

'I'm afraid I have to ask you to switch to flight mode, Mr Merchant.'

'Now?'

'The announcement was made a couple of minutes ago.'

'Brad. Give Eve this number. Look after them…'

The stewardess was standing over him, sympathetic but emphatic. He didn't bother with flight mode, just switched it off and put it away because there was nothing to see.

There were no vids of his little girl, or pictures of her with his dad, or playing on the beach.

No picture of Eve with paint on her cheek, of the two of them with Daisy, or dancing at the Nymba party.

Forget GPS. This felt like the Dark Ages.

CHAPTER SIXTEEN

THEY WERE SEA TRIALS, not a race and so not newsworthy. Eve checked the blog at least twice a day, but all the teams were cagey about revealing their times, their strategies and the only big news was that Kit, having cut short his honeymoon, was back.

He'd lost his phone, hadn't got her text and so hadn't asked what it was she'd wanted to tell him, but that was fine. Some things should be said face-to-face. It would wait.

His phone had been handed in at the airport and returned to her, but he'd picked up a new one at the airport and, having asked her to send him some photographs, said to hang onto it.

He called every morning to talk to Hannah in what, for them, was the late afternoon.

And, because he knew that she worried, he texted her a GIF of a red admiral butterfly every evening—long before dawn in Nantucket—so that when she woke up, she would know that he was safely back in harbour.

She didn't wait until morning, of course. The beep of his text was enough to wake her. Then one night she just woke. There had been no beep, no butterfly. It wasn't yet time but, wide awake and full of apprehension, she checked the team blog, then the news.

She made tea, checked again and waited. The newsflash about a freak storm hitting the Southern Ocean began to scroll across the screen just after four and she knew, deep in her heart, that he was in the middle of it.

She called Kit's phone, but it went to straight to voicemail and she was already throwing stuff into a bag when her own phone rang. It was a call from the team office, hoping to catch her before she saw on the news that Kit, putting the new keel through a test, had been caught by the storm.

It was only confirmation of what she'd known, but she still had to hang on to the wardrobe door, her body like ice, her teeth chattering as she said, 'Tell me you have contact?'

'Not at the moment, Mrs Merchant. The storm is interfering with the signals... The navy have dispatched a ship to the area. I'll call you as soon as I have more news.'

'No. I'm coming there... I'll be on the first available plane,' she said, cutting the woman off when she tried to suggest it would be better to wait. She needed to call Brad and warn him before his mother saw the news.

'Do you want to leave Hannah with us?' he asked.

'No, I want her to be the first thing Kit sees...' She broke off.

'He'll be okay, Eve,' he said, but he couldn't hide the shake in his own voice. 'I'll organise the flights and call you back.'

She monitored the news until she had to switch her phone to flight mode, checking again once they reached Boston, but there was nothing.

The journey seemed endless. They had a three-hour layover in Dubai, where there was still no news, and it was nearly thirty hours after they left Boston before they arrived in Sydney.

They were met at the gate and whisked through immigration and customs by airport staff and at the gate by a representative from the sponsor, who booked them into a hotel and then took them to the quayside office.

The staff did their best to keep the press away from them, but they had managed to get pictures of the wedding and the headlines were inevitable.

New Bride Waits for News...

They dredged up the drama of his round-the-world race, Kit's reputation for recklessness, everything she had ever dreaded. It read like an obituary, not just for him, but his team.

There were other families there. Partners, parents, children. They walked along the quay, eyes constantly scanning the horizon, drank so much coffee that they were all wired, ate food brought by the sponsors, all the time trying to ignore the press pack gathered to take photographs and stick microphones under their noses at the first sniff of disaster.

Needing some peace, Eve slipped away with Hannah, to choose an ice cream from a vendor who refused to take any money for it and found a quiet spot to sit for a while.

The clouds above them had been torn to shreds but Venus shone bright in the early evening sky. Kit could navigate by the stars, she told herself. He'd climbed a mast with broken fingers and lashed it together.

Men who could stand on a platform moving at fifty miles an hour were not mere mortals...

She heard someone running, calling her name. 'Eve! They're back!'

'What?'

And then she saw it, bent out of shape, the huge wing sail a tattered wreck, but moving under its own power towards the quay.

Everyone surged forward as the crew disembarked one by one. Bruised, battered but grinning to be scooped up by family and friends.

Kit was the last to leave and as he stepped down everyone parted to let him through. He had a gash on his cheek, a massive bruise on his forearm, black hollows beneath his eyes, but he had never looked more perfect as he encircled her with his arms, picked her up and, without a word, kissed her.

There were flashes as the press filled their boots, clapping from everyone standing on the quay, his crew, their families, a chorus of hoots from craft in the harbour, saluting the man who had brought them all back safe.

'I can't believe you're here,' he said, when he'd set her down.

'I love you, Kit. Where else would I be?'

He drew her back into his arms. 'I swear I'll never put you through that again.'

She clung to him for a moment, but then pulled back, shook her head. 'I knew who you were when I married you, but there'll be no more long-distance phone calls or night-time texts. We'll stay while you get your yacht back up and running. While you race.' She put her hands on either side of his dear battered face and said, 'I love you, just as you are, Kit Merchant. All I ask is that you keep coming home safe.'

'Daddy...'

He looked at Eve for a long time.

'Daddy!' Hannah tugged on his pants and he finally glanced down.

'Hey, there, little Puddleduck.' He bent and picked her up in one arm, keeping the other around Eve. 'If you look in my bag you'll find Ellie.'

'Ellie?'

'She's a little elephant that belonged to your mama when she was a little girl.'

Hannah retrieved the grey velvet elephant and hugged her. 'She smells like Mama.'

'That's because she hugged her so much. She's very precious and I want you to look after her for me.'

'For always?'

'For always.' He turned back to Eve. 'I don't need her, any more.'

'Kit, no.'

'Eve, yes. Out there, imagining that I might never see you again, or Hannah, I finally experienced the visceral, mind-numbing fear that my family went through when I did the round-the-world race. That you went through because you were carrying my child. What you all must have been feeling for the last couple of days. You and all these people,' he said, looking at the families hugging his crew. 'The storm came out of nowhere, slammed into us, ripping away the communications, driving us out to sea. It's a miracle we didn't lose anyone overboard.'

'How did your keel hold up?' she asked.

'The keel saved us, but I could never race to the limit again, Eve. I have too much to lose. And if you can't there is no point. It's over.'

'I'm so sorry.'

'Don't be. It's the easiest decision ever, next to marrying you. But I should call my mother. What time is it in Nantucket?'

Eve swallowed. 'It makes no difference, Kit. She'll be awake.'

He called his mother, reassured her that he was fine, handed the phone to Eve so that she could reassure her again.

'He's bruised, battered and stinks. Apart from that he's absolutely perfect.' She ended the call but didn't give him back the phone. Instead she put it in her pocket. 'You need a shower and ten hours' sleep.'

'Did I say I love you, Eve? Not just because you're Hannah's mom, but you.'

'You did just fine,' she said.

'Did I? It should have been the first thing I said. It was all I could think about saying when we were out there, but when I saw you waiting for me it was like that first day after winter, when the sun feels warm. I love you, Eve, more than I knew was possible. I didn't need Ellie out there. You were with me every minute, your smile, your warmth and I want all that, every day, and you beside me when I wake up for the rest of my life.'

'You've got it.'

He touched her face with gritty, filthy fingers and then he said, 'Who's looking after Mungo?'

'Lucy offered to move into the cottage while we're away.'

'So there's no need to rush back. Let's rent a place on the beach for a few weeks, just the three of us, and make the most of the Australian spring.'

'I'd like that. And then, when we go home, we'll start looking for a puppy.'

The opening of the Matthew Grainger Clinic was a very special occasion.

Matt's sister, Lucy, who made a moving speech about how easy it was for anyone to slip into opiate addiction, thanked everyone for their generous donations. The new diamond flashed on her finger as she unveiled a plaque to commemorate the opening.

'I felt like the Queen, swishing back that little curtain,' she said.

Brad hugged her. 'You are *my* queen.'

Eve, aware that Brad had waited until that weekend to propose in order to take her mind off today, said, 'Have you set a date for the wedding?'

'We thought Christmas,' Lucy said. 'Christmas weddings are so special but I'm going to need a little Christmas elf to help me through the day. I was hoping Hannah would be here so that I could ask if she could handle that.'

'She's having a sleepover with her cousins tonight, but I can confidently predict that she will be thrilled to be your elf.'

'And you, Eve. Will you be my matron of honour?'

'Oh, Lucy, bless your heart, I'd be so pleased to do that for you. Thank you for asking me. Is there anything I can do to help?'

'You can come dress shopping with me. Your dress was so perfect.'

'We'll take Martha with us. She's the one with the great taste.'

'That would be wonderful. My to-do list is shrinking by the minute,' she said, her eyes a touch too bright. 'I just wish Matt was here to give me away.'

Eve knew how tough it was to have that kind of gap at her wedding; she handed her a tissue, gave her a hug and said, 'Why don't you ask Kit?'

'Brad is going to want him as his best man.'

'Brad would give you the moon if it would make you happy.'

She smiled. 'I always wanted a big sister and you are just perfect, Eve. I'll go and find Brad and ask him.'

'What was that all about?' Kit asked, joining her.

'I've just volunteered you to give Lucy away. She's off to ask Brad to release you from best man duties.'

'I'm sure he'd rather have one of his own friends organise his stag.'

'I don't recall you having one,' she said. 'Or was it something so down and dirty that it was never to be spoken of?'

'Brad offered to lead me astray, but I told him I'd rather spend the time with you.'

She looked at him askance. 'Painting Hannah's bedroom?'

He grinned. 'Doing anything.' He took her

arm. 'Have you seen the auction photographs Laura curated? We're up there with Daisy.'

'We?' She looked at the board. 'How did that happen? I gave her the one with just me and Daisy. That one is…'

'Me looking at you as if I want to eat you.'

'Yes, that,' she said. 'Besides you've no right to be there. You didn't bid on the auction.'

'Neither did Philippe d'Usay, an old friend of mine who hosted Jenna Brown on a trip to the South of France. From the look of this photograph I'd say they are very close.'

'And look at this one.' She checked the name. '"Maya Talbot, in a gondola with Vittorio Rameri."'

'He looks very happy.'

'And so does she.'

They looked at some of the other photographs and then Eve spotted another couple. '"Molly Quinn with fellow guest Eric Chambault, enjoying a moment together while whale-watching."'

'He actually bid on the auction,' Kit said. 'She beat him at the last moment but he decided to go anyway. I'm sure it was pure chance they went the same week.'

She laughed. 'Perhaps, but there must have been something in the air that night. Brad should organise another event, not on such an epic scale, but special evenings out in exciting locations with those extra touches that money can't buy. He could hold it on Valentine's Day.'

'It sounds like a great idea. He's always looking for new ideas, although he's still a man down and he might be pushed for someone to organise it.'

'What does it involve?'

'Finding people to donate the prizes is the biggest job. Mom did a great job with the opioid clinic auction, but she and Dad are planning a cruise early in the spring, Laura is back at uni and Lucy is completely absorbed in designing a boat adapted for teaching disabled kids to sail.'

'And organising her wedding. I do like her, Kit. I hope she and Brad will be happy.'

'He is wearing the glazed expression of a man who is head over heels. The same look I see in the mirror every morning.'

She leaned against him. He still smelled of

the sea, but these days there were overtones of puppy.

'It's great to see you two comfortable together, too, but it occurs to me that if the resort is short a Merchant—in other words you,' she said, 'I should step into the breach. I'm only teaching two mornings a week so there's no reason why I can't organise a Valentine's Day auction.'

'I can think of one very good reason. The house is straight. We have a spare bedroom and I thought, since you have time to spare, that it might be fun to start working on a project that Hannah has her heart set on.'

'Oh? What's that?'

'We wrote a letter to Santa and she put a baby sister at the top of her list.'

'Oh.' She blushed then laughed. 'That would be fun, but you're forgetting something. I'm a woman—'

'No,' he said, his arms around her waist, drawing her close, 'I definitely haven't forgotten that.'

'I'm a woman and we can multitask, but even I can't deliver a baby in time for Christmas. And she might have to take a brother.'

'She was adamant that it had to be a sister. We might have to keep working on it until we get it right.'

'I'm up for that. Shall we skip the buffet, go home and start working on it?'

* * * * *

LET'S TALK
Romance

For exclusive extracts, competitions
and special offers, find us online:

f facebook.com/millsandboon

⊙ @millsandboonuk

🐦 @millsandboon

Or get in touch on 0844 844 1351*

For all the latest titles coming soon,
visit millsandboon.co.uk/nextmonth

*Calls cost 7p per minute plus your phone company's price per
minute access charge

Want even more
ROMANCE?

Join our bookclub today!